THE
KEY OF
ZORGEN

THE
KEY OF
ZORGEN

Lynette Bishop

Scripture Union
130 City Road, London EC1V 2NJ.

By the same author
Escape from Gehalla

Phototypeset by Input Typesetting Ltd, London
Printed and bound in Great Britain by Cox and Wyman
Ltd, Reading

Chapter one

High in the lonely castle turret the midnight shadows threw the small room into sudden darkness, as clouds like great bat wings flew across the night sky and cut off the light of the moon.

Kate, in the act of lifting a stone slab in the centre of the dusty floor, gave a groan of impatience. She groped for her lantern and felt instead the soft, sleek coat of Mig as she rubbed against Kate, a rumbling purr beginning deep in her throat. Mig was a Mondarian she-cat as big as a tiger, with the powerful body of a panther, the agility of a lynx and the mentality of an overgrown kitten. She had been given to Kate when she was a small cub. Her whole world revolved around Kate.

'Mig, will you get out of the way!' exclaimed Kate in annoyance. 'I'm trying to light the lantern. I've got to find the note and get back to my room before Marise does. You know there'll be trouble if she finds I'm gone.'

Mig's amber eyes stared dolefully at Kate. She lifted her haunches and moved away, the picture of dejection. She had learned that when Kate spoke in that sharp tone of voice, Mig, large as she was, had best make herself invisible. She tried to blend her large, black shape into the deeper blackness of the room. Her velvet hind paw came into contact with something hard that rolled and clattered noisily across the stone floor. With a whine of distress Mig bounded away from it and cowered in the corner.

'Good girl, Mig,' cried Kate. 'You've found the lantern!' Mig pricked up her ears and looked in surprise at the shadowy figure that was Kate. The room flared suddenly into a pale light which set the shadows dancing.

Kate, with her long, red hair tumbling over her shoulders and the skirts of her green gown trailing in the dust, was busily tackling the flagstone again.

'Yes, there *is* a note!' she announced in triumph, drawing out a folded sheet of white paper from the cavity under the stone. 'Right, Mig,' she said, settling the flagstone back into place and leaping to her feet. 'Let's get back to the west wing. Then we can see what we have here.' She tapped the note, patted Mig on the head and moved to the window.

The clouds were finally clearing the moon, freeing its pale light to flood the garden and pour a shimmering gloss of silver over the castle walls. Kate gripped the cold stone of the window-sill and leaned forward, her hair blowing in soft tendrils against her cheeks in the cool night breeze.

'One night,' she said to Mig, 'he might come to see if I collect the note. Whoever's sending these notes . . .'

Kate stopped abruptly and her green eyes widened. In the shadow of the keep she thought she saw another shadow move. She leaned out as far as she dared, straining to see.

Mig, perplexed by Kate's actions, felt she should try and see what it was that was making Kate behave so strangely. She raised herself up on her hind legs and planted her large, black paws on the window-sill next to Kate's slender hands. The stone slab of the window-sill shifted, then, a split second later, went crashing to the ground. Kate felt the blood rush to her head. The ground swam crazily below as she felt herself losing her balance, tipping over the broken sill. She screamed.

Mig, who had grasped Kate's belt of linked copper chains in her teeth, was startled by the scream and almost let go. But by then the impetus of Mig's tug at the belt had taken them both tumbling backwards. They fell together onto the stone floor of the turret.

Kate, for once speechless, sat up dizzily, holding one hand to her head and clutching the note in the other.

'The light,' she groaned, and pulled herself shakily to her feet. Mig watched, her head cocked to one side as Kate crossed to the lantern and blew it out. 'No one must see the light,' she explained. 'No one must know we're here.'

Cautiously Kate moved to the window. As she had feared, the noise of the crashing stone had caught the attention of the guard on night-watch. Hurrying across the gardens to the east tower came three figures, their gaze focused on the turret window. Kate drew back quickly, her heart beating fast. Their upturned faces, ghostly white in the moonlight, had shown Kate who they were. One, as she had expected, wore the bronze-plated armour of the guard on night watch. But Kate was startled, for the wearer was Armard, who she had thought was at this moment keeping a secret rendezvous with Kate's lady-in-waiting, Marise. More alarming still was the fact that with him came Ricaldan, the Captain of the Guard and Edric, her father's steward.

The sight of Edric made Kate's heart quake for Kate was answerable to Edric for her behaviour during the weeks that her father was away at a peace conference in the north of Mondar. If he was in a good mood Edric would make her feel as if she were three years old not thirteen. He would look down his long nose at her and say, 'Princess Katherine, if there was something you needed from the east turret,' (which he knew there was not) 'you should have asked Marise to instruct one of the servants to fetch it.' Kate did not dare to think what he might do if he was angry. She had seen the cold depths in his pale eyes and she had heard tales of prisoners questioned by Edric who screamed and pleaded to be allowed to die. Her father had laughed when she had asked him about it. When he saw that she took it seriously, he had been angry and had said she should not believe lies and slander about a good man.

Kate paused only a minute by the window as questions and suspicions raced through her mind. Then she strode swiftly across the room in the path of the moonlight and, reaching for the bracket high in the turret wall, pulled hard on it. A section of the wall slowly opened. Kate tapped her foot impatiently. Whether Edric was the evil man she suspected him to be or not, she had no intention of waiting to find out. As soon as the opening in the wall became wide enough, Kate slipped through, bundling Mig in front of her. Only when it had completely closed behind her did she let out her breath in a long sigh of relief. She was in the tunnel. She was safe.

The secret tunnel was an unusual one. It led under the ramparts linking each of the four turrets.

'Bother!' Kate exclaimed into the darkness. She clamped her hand over her mouth as the word echoed along the tunnel as if it was peopled with small creatures, each with a peevish complaint to make. It was only as total darkness closed in around her that Kate realised she had left the lantern inside the turret room.

It would take only minutes to slip back inside, fetch the lantern and close the opening again, but she was not sure how quickly Edric and his companions would reach the room. She did not know if she had those few minutes.

Kate leaned against the wall and strained to catch the least hint of sound from the room beyond. She heard nothing. She lifted her hand to the bracket and listened again. 'What shall I do, Mig?' she whispered. Mig stood helpless in the dark, her tail down. 'I'll risk it,' said Kate with sudden determination. But she had hesitated too long, for even as she closed both hands round the bracket, she heard the faint sound of voices and rapid footsteps on the stone stairs.

Kate let the bracket go as if it was on fire and reached out to touch Mig. Her hand made contact with Mig's soft fur and she bent to whisper in Mig's pricked up ear. 'Stay still and be very, very quiet, Mig, there's a good girl.' Then Kate leaned against the wall, listening hard.

She wanted to find out if they suspected that she had been in the turret – in fact if they had any idea that she paid regular visits there. She also hoped that she might overhear something which would give her a clue to the identity of the writer of the anonymous notes she had been receiving over the past weeks.

At first she was disappointed because she could hardly hear anything. There were two voices, one high and sharp that she recognised as Edric's. The other was deep and assertive – Ricaldan's. She supposed they had left Armard at the foot of the tower to keep watch. To her surprise, as she got used to the distortion in the voices caused by the thickness of the walls, she found she could make out a word here and there, then parts of sentences.

'No one,' boomed Ricaldan.

'No one!' came back Edric's voice scathingly.

Kate bit her lips as she heard Edric say '. . . hiding somewhere . . .' If they were to touch the bracket! Then Edric's voice grew fainter and Kate imagined he had perhaps crossed to the window. 'Danger from Dolan . . .' came Ricaldan's voice, surprisingly loud and close. Then Edric said something she could not catch and in reply Ricaldan said, 'He couldn't possibly suspect.' After that his voice grew fainter and Kate thought perhaps they were leaving the room. 'Who couldn't suspect?' she wondered.

'Will Bedien . . . ?' asked Ricaldan. Kate jumped as she heard her father's name, then froze as she heard Edric laugh in reply. It was a cruel laugh, without humour, but it was not the laughter that made Kate's cheeks turn pale in the darkness of the tunnel. It was because, as he laughed, Edric said something of which Kate only caught two words: '. . . with Kate . . .' The feeling held in those two words of danger threatening her was so great that Kate almost missed the next words. It was probably only because they were the last two words spoken before the silence fell that they registered at all. Ricaldan, it seemed, was angered by whatever it was that Edric had just said for his words came loudly and clearly; 'Of course we'll get the key!'

When they had gone Kate found she was trembling. She hugged Mig who was sitting, puzzled but patient, in the dark tunnel. The warmth of the big cat comforted Kate but she felt stunned, unable to gather her confused wits. She felt strongly that she had overhead something which, if only she could piece it together, was vitally important – perhaps a matter of life and death for herself, for her father Bedien and for the destiny of their kingdom, Mondar.

Kate fingered the gold chain round her neck. 'We'll get the key,' Ricaldan had said. Kate shivered for she knew which key he meant and also what it meant for that key to fall into the wrong hands. The Key of Zorgen was made of fine gold set with three small but perfect gems – a sapphire, a ruby and a topaz. Its importance did not lie in its beauty or its value but in its significance. For the Key of Zorgen was entrusted to the ruler of Mondar. As long as he held the key, the kingdom could not be taken out of his hands.

A new cause for alarm came to Kate's mind as she puzzled over Ricaldan's words. When Bedien had set out for the peace conference he had done something which, if Kate had thought about it at the time, would have struck her as unusual. He had called Kate into his apartments and, taking her hands in his, had said, 'Kate, I want you to look after something.' Kate remembered how he had cupped his hand under her chin and tilted her face so that his brown eyes were able to search her green ones. 'Zorgen will be with you, Kate,' he had said. Kate shrugged at the words. Her father was always saying Zorgen this and Zorgen that. Kate did not feel that this talk of Zorgen meant anything. She waited impatiently to find out what he wanted her to look after.

'Kate,' he had said, reaching for a silk bag from inside his doublet. 'No one is to know that you have this – not Edric, not the Council of Zorgen, not Marise. No one. I want everyone to think I have taken it with me.' He had opened the bag and tipped out into her upturned palms an exquisite object, gleaming gold with dark blue, deep red and amber lights. Kate had raised incredulous eyes to his. Bedien had nodded. 'Yes. The Key of Zorgen.'

Slowly Kate unclasped the chain holding the key from around her neck. She had carried it with her, hidden for safety. Now, after what she had heard, she felt it was no longer safe with her. She released the pendant gently until she had it in her hand, gleaming even in the blackness of the tunnel, the Key of Zorgen.

'What shall we do, Mig?' she asked, feeling the burden was too heavy for her to carry alone. Mig licked Kate's hand, unable to understand the cause of her distress, but at least able to show sympathy. Then Kate brightened. 'We can hide it here, Mig. It's perfect. Nobody knows about this tunnel except us. Come on. Help me dig a hole and we'll put a stone or something for a marker.'

To Mig's surprise and delight Kate began scrabbling in the rough, stone earth of the tunnel floor. 'Come on, Mig, help,' urged Kate. Mig did not need to be asked twice. The hole was soon deep enough to hide the Key of Zorgen. It was quickly filled in and covered with pebbles and stones. Kate felt around until she found a stone she would remember, sharp and pointed on one face, smooth and flat on the other. She placed it where they had dug the hole, then rose stiffly to her feet.

She wiped dirty hands on the sides of her dress and stood for a moment undecided. Finally she said, 'Mig,

I don't think we'll risk going back for the lantern. Are you game to find our way back along the tunnel in the dark?' Mig, who had been licking her paw and thinking of the warmth of the hearth in Kate's room and a bowl of tasty meat, wondered what mad scheme Kate was suggesting now. She lowered her tail with a show of resignation and padded along reluctantly behind Kate.

Kate had plenty of time as she groped her way along the dark, squelchy tunnel, to decide what she would do if she was caught by Marise when they reached her apartments. She would like to confide in someone but could she trust Marise when she had seen Armard with Edric and Ricaldan? She knew someone she felt she could trust – the writer of the anonymous notes, which had cheered her with their offers of friendship, encouragement and advice. But she had no idea who the writer was or where she could find him.

Kate stopped abruptly so that Mig, close on her heels, bumped into her. 'How stupid!' she exclaimed. 'I've left the note behind. Mig, I've left the note I came all this way to fetch by the entrance to the tunnel!' Mig sensed that Kate's outburst was not directed at Mig but at Kate herself and purred. 'Well, I can't go back now,' sighed Kate. 'We'll go back tomorrow – with a lantern.'

To Kate's relief she and Mig reached the apartments without meeting anyone. Mig went straight to her long-awaited bowl of meat while Kate quickly washed and changed into her night-gown. She stuffed the green dress with its tell-tale stains of mud and dirt under her bed and climbed in between the soft sheets. She was fast asleep when Marise peered round the bedroom door.

It was in the long, dark hours between midnight and dawn that Kate began to dream. She saw Edric standing in the turret room. She was no longer safe in the tunnel but trapped between the secret opening and the wall. Edric was laughing and the harsh vengeful sound echoed round the room. 'With Kate,' he said. 'With Kate.' He laughed again and Kate saw that he had something

14

clasped in his hand. The Key of Zorgen, she thought in alarm. Then she saw that it was not the key but a piece of crumpled paper.

'You should have read the note,' Edric cackled. 'It might have saved you.' His eyes burned fiercely as he pointed his finger at her and said in a quiet voice of doom. 'Nothing can save you now.'

'No,' screamed Kate. 'No.' But Edric took her by the shoulders and began to shake her and shake her.

'Kate! Kate, wake up,' came the voice sharply. Kate opened her eyes and saw Marise sitting on her bed, her hands on Kate's shoulders. 'It's all right, Kate,' she murmured soothingly 'You've been having a nightmare. But everything's all right now.'

Kate looked at Marise's face, full of concern, but Edric's face with the intense, burning eyes floated in front of her. No, thought Kate. It's not all right. It's not all right at all. I don't know what it is exactly but something is very wrong.

Chapter two

Debbie had wanted to be alone so she had left them all to it and come for a walk along the cliff-top. She walked until the village and the small estate of new houses were out of sight, then dropped down onto the warm grass and sat hugging her knees, looking out to sea.

It was a perfect day — Debbie's first day in Polmar. There was hardly a cloud in the blue sky and the sea was also blue, deepening to green. Seagulls circled overhead and small boats with white sails bobbed on the water far below. Debbie stared at the horizon and the scene blurred, sky melting into sea, as tears of anger and disappointment stung her eyes.

'Cornwall! It's really smashing there. Lucky you!' her friends had said.

'Polmar's quite pretty, Debbie. You'll feel differently when you see it,' her mother had told her. But Debbie felt homesick for London, as she had known she would before they moved.

Polmar was pretty and no doubt Cornwall was very interesting, but that didn't help now. Nothing about this alien place filled the ache for the familiar, friendly East End.

Debbie clasped her hands more tightly round the

rough denim of her jeans. 'It's just not fair!' she said.

What made it worse was that no one else really understood how she felt, how much she loved London even with all its faults. Who in their right minds would prefer living in grimy, noisy London when they could move to Cornwall with its picturesque villages, sandy beaches and mysterious legends? Not that there had been any choice about going. Her father had been vicar of St Luke's for ten years now. She had known that he would move on to a new church sooner or later. It was just that she hadn't expected it to be now — not when she had only just finished her first year at Wood Lane, settled down and made good friends. The thought of starting at a new school in a few weeks time did not bear thinking about.

The sun was high in the sky and Debbie began to feel its heat burning through her thin, pink T-shirt. Her brown ponytail hung limply from its white band. She was beginning to feel hot and sticky. It wouldn't be like this at home, she thought, unreasonably.

As she looked along the headland Debbie saw two specks in the distance moving towards her. She stared in growing dismay as one speck grew larger and quickly resolved itself into a fast moving mass of shaggy white fur. There was no mistaking their Old English sheepdog. It was Robert and Chumley. No doubt Robert had been sent to fetch her.

Chumley arrived in style. He threw himself at Debbie, treating her to enthusiastic licks of his tongue as if he had not seen her for months. Robert came more slowly, running on podgy legs across the tufted grass of the headland. When he finally reached her, red-faced and with his glasses misting up, Debbie felt guilty for making him come all this way. Despite the fact that Robert was her brother and was two years younger, she was fond of him and they got on very well together.

'Debbie,' said Robert, panting for breath. 'Debbie, you've got to . . . come . . . now. Quickly.'

Debbie smiled. Robert didn't look capable of putting one foot in front of the other, let alone hurrying all the way back to the village. Chumley, on the other hand, looked as if he could go all the way along the coast to Trewythrin and still not get out of breath.

'Sit down a minute and get your breath back,' suggested Debbie, patting a place beside her.

Robert opened his mouth to protest, realised how hot and tired he was, and sank thankfully onto the grass next to his sister. The three of them sat companionably for a while in silence, brother and sister gazing out to sea and Chumley pretending complete disdain of the seagulls overhead.

Debbie began to feel better with Robert and Chumley sitting there beside her, the warmth of the sun washing through her and the sea stretching away into the unknown, holding the promise of new and exciting discoveries to be made.

They sat in silence for a few minutes more, neither of them wanting to break the spell of the balmy summer afternoon. Then Robert, beginning to feel his conscience pricking him, said reluctantly, 'We ought to go. We've got visitors — people from our new church. There's a girl your age and another smaller one,' he pulled a face, ' — that they want me to play with!'

'Oh,' said Debbie flatly and the agony of having to make new friends gripped her afresh. The only thing worse than having to find a friend was having to be friendly with someone your parents thought you ought to get along with. This was going to be so embarrassing . . .

Their house was not in the old village with its picturesque stone cottages and gardens ablaze with fuchsias, roses and honeysuckle, but on the new estate which had small fenced gardens with neat, square lawns. It had not had any time to develop any character of its own, not like their rambling vicarage in London with its sprawling garden, full of hidden places behind bushes and under old trees.

To Debbie's relief the visitors had gone when they arrived home. Instead there were the comfortable noises of her mother in the kitchen with the radio on and her father hammering away upstairs.

'Never mind,' said her mother, boiling the kettle for a cup of tea. We're invited round there for tea on Saturday. You can meet them then.'

'Oh,' said Debbie, catching Robert's eye as he pulled a face. 'That will be . . . nice.'

Her mother smiled and stepped out into the hall. 'Ian,' she called, 'cup of tea!' The hammering stopped abruptly and the house settled into a cosy, sunlit silence.

The next day it rained. And the day after that. Grey Cornish clouds hung over the small estate, making it look bleak and drab. Debbie stared gloomily into the garden. 'Well,' said her mother, 'at least we can get the house straight without being tempted to spend the day sunbathing.'

On Friday morning the sun shone again, as if it had decided to put in an appearance for the weekend. The sky was as brilliant a blue as it had been on the first day but now the colours of everything outside — of each petal, leaf and blade of grass — seemed brighter, fresh from the two days of rain, and the air carried the scent of summer flowers. Debbie had to admit that, with cushions and curtains softening the bright, modern rooms and the light gilding the familiar, old furniture, the house looked cosy and welcoming. When her father suggested that they take a drive out in the car to explore their new surroundings, she found herself actually looking forward to the day ahead.

It's a bit like being on a sea-saw, Debbie thought as she munched through a cheese roll at Polmar Tor. 'One minute I hate being here and the next something happens which makes me think I'm going to like it after all.'

She liked the look of the rocky plateau where they had stopped for a picnic lunch. It was a local beauty spot with a ruined castle perched on the cliff-top. The grey rock and the crumbling stone of the castle ruins were a dramatic contrast to the green grass, blue sky and emerald sea. She was itching to explore the ruins. She gulped down a beaker of orangeade, helped herself to a chocolate bar and an apple, then got to her feet.

'I'm going to explore. Coming?' she asked Robert. Chumley leapt up, tongue hanging out and tail wagging, but Robert stayed hunched over the pocket electronic game he was playing.

'I'll come in a minute,' he mumbled.

The ruins were, for the most part, covered with grass, but you could still see the broken outline of what must once have been a huge castle. There was really nothing to explore. No part of the original building remained intact. Chumley lost interest and raced away to look for something more exciting. Debbie looked around her, disappointed that there was no feeling of the mysterious past. It was hard to imagine that this had ever been a place where people had lived; where ladies in long dresses had sat at their tapestries, perhaps looking out to sea; where knights had fought; where minstrels had sung songs of high romance and daring deeds. Debbie sighed. Ahead of her was a steeply sloping mound with a flat stone at its top. She climbed it and sat gingerly on the warm stone to eat her chocolate and munch her apple.

When she had finished eating there was still no sign of Robert. Now she felt thirsty again. She thought she might as well go back. She stooped to pick up a handful of small stones to play a game with later and her eye was drawn to a crumpled piece of paper wedged in the shelter of two mossy stones. Probably a piece of litter she told herself but, pocketing the stones, she reached out to pick it up anyway.

It had yellowed and was slightly brittle to her touch. Curiously she unfolded it and saw to her surprise that it was covered with writing in a strange script. At first she wasn't sure it was English then, as she peered at it, like the word games in a puzzle book, the meaning suddenly became clear.

Princess Katherine,

Beware. Dolan seeks the key. Do not trust Edric or Marise. Enemies surround you. But I remain always,

Your friend,

G.

Debbie stared at it frowning. A shiver ran through her. The old, yellowed note with its strange message made her feel both excited and afraid. She could hardly wait to show Robert what she had found. She picked up the note along with her sweet paper and apple core and made her way back down.

Robert looked up when she arrived. 'Just one more go,' he said and hunched over his game again.

Debbie's excitement died as Robert turned away from her. He hadn't even looked at her properly. The news had been on the tip of her tongue but she could see Robert wasn't listening. If that stupid electronic game was more important than a mysterious note which might be hundreds of years old, then she wouldn't bother him with her discovery.

But who else could she tell? Not her parents. They would probably show some interest but they might also be practical about it and explain away the mystery. If they had still been in London there were friends she could have told. Here there was no one. She would just have to keep her discovery to herself. The decision made her uneasy for some reason.

'I've been to the ruins now,' said Debbie, pushing the note into her pocket and dropping her rubbish into the bag her mother had provided for leftovers. 'There's nothing worth seeing.' She wandered off as casually as possible to the edge of the cliff and took out the note again. A sudden breeze caught the edge of the fragile paper and almost whipped it out of her hand. Her heart missed a beat. She gripped the paper more tightly.

In that moment that she nearly lost it Debbie knew how important the note was. Not just because it was old and probably valuable, but because she felt that somehow she had been meant to find it. She folded the note carefully and put it away in her pocket. As she did so her fingers touched the small hoard of stones and she drew them out, grasping them tightly in her fist. She felt cross. Cross with Robert because he had not been interested when he should have been. Cross with her parents for bringing her away from friends she usually shared things with. Even cross with Katherine and whoever had put the note there for leaving her with a mystery she couldn't possibly solve.

Her hand was hurting. One of the stones, though flat on one side, was sharply pointed on the other and was digging into her palm. She took it and flung it out as far as she could into the sparkling sea. She wished for the hundredth time that she was back home in London again and that everything was just as it had been before.

Chapter three

Kate slept late and woke hungry. Sunlight poured in through the high arched windows and washed the whole room in warm shades of summer. It added golden depths to the yellow silk of her sheets before dancing through the leafy trees of the tapestry on the wall. Last night's dream and the adventure in the turret seemed unreal. Kate pushed the memories aside. She had always been told that she let her imagination run away with her. It had probably been the effect of the summer storm, the moonlight and the dark shadows of the tunnel. She swung her legs over the edge of the bed and felt for her slippers. She was certainly not going to let any wild imaginings about Edric spoil her day.

The slippers were not there. Kate bent down and, groping under her bed, came across the soiled dress she had thrust there the night before. The door opened and Marise came in, smiling, with the sunlight highlighting her coiled braids of golden hair like a crown. Quickly Kate pulled out her slippers, at the same time pushing the tell-tale dress out of sight.

'How are you feeling this morning, Kate?' asked Marise, concern shadowing her violet eyes.

'I'm fine, thank you, Marise,' Kate replied, smiling

brightly. 'But I'm really hungry. And eager to be out,' she added, moving to the window. 'I think maybe I'll take a ride to the Far Woods. Come with me. It will be fun.'

Kate thought she saw a glimmer of unease in Marise's eyes but she replied quite quickly, 'All right. It's a lovely day. I'll just get your breakfast first.'

Kate stared at the door as it closed softly behind Marise. There was something in Marise's behaviour that puzzled her. She shrugged and moved to the carved oak chest to choose something suitable to wear for riding. Perhaps she should try and talk with Marise, find out if anything was worrying her — though if it was a lovers' tiff with Armard, Kate would have no idea what to do about that.

As she pulled her night-gown off, Kate forgot all about Marise's problems, real or imagined, and was filled with sudden panic. The Key of Zorgen, always hanging on its gold chain round her neck, was no longer there. Of course, she remembered, she had buried it last night in the tunnel. Then Edric's words and his grim face came to her vividly. She knew then that it was not her imagination running wild. The sunshine could not banish the cold reality of what had happened last night.

By the time Marise brought Kate's breakfast, her appetite had completely deserted her. So had her enthusiasm for the ride. Mig came bounding in after Marise and Kate was grateful for the distraction as the large cat nuzzled up to Kate, purring with pleasure.

'I can see you've had your breakfast!' Kate laughed, stroking the large, black head. Mig's liquid amber eyes fixed dotingly on her and Kate began to feel a little better. After all, she was not alone. She had Mig. And then there was Marise. Kate's eyes turned thoughtfully to Marise who was setting her breakfast out on a small table by the window. Perhaps she could confide in Marise? After all the fact that Armard had been with Edric and Ricaldan last night really meant nothing. It

24

certainly did not mean that Marise could not be trusted.

'Marise,' she began, but her voice was drowned in a sudden burst of birdsong through the window and Marise straightened without having heard.

'I'll just go and get ready,' Marise said, moving to the door. She paused in the doorway. 'Unless there's anything else you need.'

'Yes,' Kate began again, then faltered, suddenly unsure of herself. 'No. You go and get ready,' Marise looked at her uncertainly. 'I'm quite anxious to go on this ride.'

'That was a lie,' Kate confided to Mig as the door closed behind Marise. 'I don't want to go at all now. I just want to get back into the tunnel and find the note. Oh, Mig, I always seem to be getting into trouble.' She bit absentmindedly into a slice of bread spread with honey, then pushed the plate impatiently away. 'Do you think I should tell Marise, Mig?'

Mig was looking not at Kate but at the discarded breakfast. 'Well, a lot of help you are, you greedy animal. I suppose you want a second breakfast.' She set the plate on the floor and stood looking through the casement window at the rich green grounds of the castle, the tips of the trees of the Far Woods feathering the sky beyond the east turret. 'I wish Father was here. Oh, Mig, what am I going to do?'

As she rode along, Kate decided that she just could not go on trying to sort out the problem alone. She would talk to Marise. With the warmth of the sun flowing through her and the fresh wind on her face, she began to feel more confident again. They would pause for a rest when they reached the edge of the Far Woods. She would talk to Marise then.

Kate sprawled on a grassy hillock and ran her fingers through her tangled hair. Marise sat down carefully beside her, looking cool and composed, every hair of her golden braids in place. 'Marise,' she began abruptly, before she could change her mind, 'there's something I want to ask you about.'

Marise turned towards her with a smile, inviting confidences. 'Yes, Kate?'

Kate watched their horses cropping the grass nearby and struggled to find the right words. After the silence of the heath the noises of the wood behind them distracted her and made it difficult for her to think. Leaves rustled. Twigs creaked. Birds sang. Then, out of the medley of noises, one startlingly clear sound reached Kate — a burst of birdsong, piercing and sweet. Kate looked at Marise but Marise appeared to have heard nothing unusual. Her attention was completely focused on Kate.

Kate rose to her feet, stammering a little as she tried to fill in the awkward silence. 'Well, it's that . . . er . . . I . . . er . . . I just don't know how to put it.' She wandered over to a tall elm. From its branches a small, grey bird looked steadily at her with sharp, black eyes.

'Kate,' it said, 'I called you bright and early. I was beginning to think you'd never hear me.'

Kate leaned against the bark of the tree and listened. She should have realised that the burst of birdsong she had heard earlier was Fleet's signal that he wanted to talk to her. She had heard the signal often enough over the past few years, though she had not yet decided which fact surprised her the most — that she was able to hear Fleet talk or that no one else could! Marise obviously could not for she was fidgeting, trying not to look impatient. No expression registered on her face as Fleet said, 'Kate, you're in danger. Beware of Marise. Get away from here please.'

Marise an enemy! Kate's eyes widened. Marise turned to look at her and Kate without having to act too much, tried to look hesitant and confused. 'Marise, the thing I wanted to ask you was . . .' She paused to catch Fleet's final words, at the same time racking her brain for something to say. A sudden flash of inspiration struck her and she finished in a low voice '. . . about a boy.'

Marise's face cleared and she leaned forward encouragingly. 'You see,' Kate continued, warming to her subject, 'I think there's this boy who likes me and . . .'

She must have spun a good story for Kate was smothered in Marise's advice and concern for the rest of the day. It wasn't until the evening after they had dined in the great hall, that Marise left her alone. And even then Kate thought it was probably only because she had arranged to meet Armard.

'Oh, Mig,' she sighed, settling before the fire in her room. 'I've had a dreadful day. But the awful thing is that it's far from over yet. She stretched her hands out to the warmth of the flames and stared into the strange shifting landscapes of the fire. 'I've got to get away, Mig. I met Fleet in the Far Woods and he said I'm in danger.'

Mig could not understand Kate's words but she sensed that more than anything right now Kate needed a friend. She put her big black paw on Kate's knee. Kate turned to her and, almost knocking her off balance, flung her arms round her. Mig felt something damp trickle down her flank as Kate buried her face in Mig's fur. 'Oh, Mig, I'm so afraid,' Kate sobbed.

To Mig's relief Kate seemed her cheerful self after that. But then she changed her clothes and put on some strange things Mig had never seen before. Finally as she pushed all her bright hair out of sight under a cap, she did not look like Kate at all.

'Now listen, Mig,' she said, 'I want you to be very good and very quiet. We're going to the Far Woods to meet Fleet.' Mig gazed at her, trying to understand. 'But first of all we're going to the kitchen to get some food.' Mig purred, rubbing against Kate for this sounded like one of Kate's better ideas.

She followed Kate on silent, velvet paws, slinking through shadows down to the kitchens. Kate let Mig have a large chunk of the kind of meat she usually had only on special days, while she bundled up a parcel of food, small enough to be able to carry easily. Then they

27

were away through the grounds of the castle, slipping through the postern gate, heading for the dark, shadowy outline of the Far Woods.

The castle behind them rose solid and dark in the moonlight, save for the faint candle glow from windows here and there. Kate, looking back, thought she glimpsed the shining gold of Marise's hair in one window high up, but she could not be sure. She shivered and turned away to press on across the eerie headland to the silent woods.

Marise lifted her golden head from Armard's shoulder and pushed away his arms. She had been half watching through the window and now she thought she glimpsed two dark shapes on the moonlit headland. 'Yes,' she whispered as she peered through the window. 'Look, Armard, there they are.' Armard joined her at the window, slipping his arm round her shoulders.

'You were right, my clever love,' he said softly into her hair.

'Oh yes,' she replied, a note of triumph stealing into her voice. 'They suspect nothing! They think they are cleverly escaping danger, Armard. They know nothing of what we have lying in wait for them in the woods!'

At the boundary of the woods, Kate hesitated and Mig edged behind her, startled by the sudden hooting of an owl. 'I think this is where we should meet Fleet,' Kate whispered uncertainly. She took a deep breath and moved cautiously into the shadow of the wood. 'Fleet,' she called, raising her voice a little.

Mig waited uneasily in the last patch of moonlight and looked back the way they had come. As she turned away there was a sudden movement from behind trees and out of bushes. Dark shapes hurled themselves forward onto Kate.

'No!' screamed Kate. 'Help!'

Then before Mig could gather her scattered wits, the

scream was cut off and there was only the stillness and silence of the empty headland and the dark wood.

Chapter four

Debbie had got tired of throwing stones and had begun dissecting blades of grass instead. Out of the corner of her eye she could see Robert walking across the headland to join her. She decided she would show him the note after all. She was feeling much better about things now. But first she thought she would get her own back on him for spoiling the excitement of her discovery.

'Debbie!' called Robert. 'Come and look at the castle with me.'

Debbie watched the familiar, slightly tubby figure eagerly approaching and smiled.

'Robert,' she said, walking to meet him, 'there's something I need to do first but I'll meet you at the castle in ten minutes. I've got something really exciting to tell you.'

Debbie sauntered away, leaving Robert looking puzzled but pleased. When she was sure Robert could no longer see her she began running back to their picnic site. Her mother had tidied everything away and was lying on a rug reading a book. She looked up as Debbie approached breathlessly.

'Debbie, can you find Robert? Tell him we'll be going in about half an hour. Dad's taken Chumley for a walk.

I should think they'll be back by then.'

'Yes. OK,' replied Debbie, rummaging in the picnic basket.

'Debbie, what are you looking for?'

'The orangeade bottle.'

'There's none left, I'm afraid. The bottle's in that bag of rubbish.'

Debbie turned from the basket to the bag and fished out the bottle. 'I'm not thirsty. I just want to borrow the bottle,' she said, getting to her feet. 'Be back soon,' she added, hurrying away in the direction of the castle ruins.

Robert could be relied on to be on time. It was exactly ten minutes from the time Debbie had left him to the time he arrived at the ruins. Debbie waved to him from the flat stone at the top of the slope. Robert toiled up the slope and perched next to Debbie on the edge of the stone.

'Right,' he said, 'tell me.'

So Debbie told Robert about the note she had found.

'OK, let's see it!' he said.

With a flourish Debbie produced the note from her pocket. Robert looked at it with interest.

'I think,' said Debbie taking a deep breath, 'there may be something else buried underneath.'

Robert looked at her dubiously. 'There's nothing in the note about something being buried.'

'It's just a feeling I've got,' said Debbie, sensing that Robert really wanted to be convinced, despite his protest. 'I'm going to look anyway.' She began scooping the earth away, slightly to the left of the spot where she had just buried the orangeade bottle.

To her delight Robert, mumbling something about 'just a quick look,' bent to dig as well.

They had been digging for quite a while when they heard their mother's voice calling from somewhere on the other side of the ruins, 'Robert! Debbie! Time to go!'

Debbie sat back on her heels, feeling thoroughly fed up. She was hot and dirty and she had spend fifteen miserable minutes trying not to dig up the orangeade bottle while Robert moved further and further away in the wrong direction.

'Debbie,' said Robert in a hushed voice. 'I think I've found something. Come and have a look.'

That, thought Debbie, was just about the last straw! Robert had not shown any interest when she found something. Now, instead of falling for her trick, he was claiming to find something too! And what was more, the place where he had dug his hole, though Robert had no way of knowing, was very near the small crevice where Debbie had found the note and almost exactly under the spot where she had scooped up the small stones!

'What is it?' asked Debbie crossly, peering over his shoulder. Robert scraped the earth aside carefully and in the hollowed cavity he had made Debbie saw the faint glimpse of something shining like gold.

'Debbie!' her mother's voice came nearer. 'Where are you?'

Both Robert and Debbie got into trouble for getting dirty and for being late. But sitting in the back seat of the car, driving through the sunny afternoon on their way into Trewythrin, they did not mind, for they had actually found something that neither of them had expected to be there.

Robert had tried to examine their find but, as Chumley was showing too much interest, he had stuffed it back into the pocket of his shorts. From the quick glimpse he and Debbie had had as they freed it from the earth, it looked as if it might be a jewelled pendant on a chain.

'We'll have to find somewhere where you two can get cleaned up before we go anywhere else,' their mother said in exasperated tones. She turned to look at Debbie. 'I'm surprised at you at your age.' Debbie slipped further down into her seat. She caught Robert's eye. He patted his pocket and winked.

'And you had better watch your step, young man,' his father said, catching his eye in the driving mirror.

They found public toilets in the car park at Trewythrin and their mother's face brightened considerably when Robert and Debbie emerged from them once more presentable and clean.

Trewythrin was a picturesque place. There was an old church, some bright, attractive shops and a museum. As they walked they caught glimpses of cobbled streets and courtyards with tubs of geraniums giving lively splashes of colour. Turning into the main street they passed a small café with red gingham curtains and gleaming copper pots and pans in the window. 'Ian,' exclaimed Janet Matthews in delight, 'we must come back here for tea!'

They decided that they would split up and meet later for tea since Trewythrin was not too big and no one could get lost.

The first suggestion was that Debbie go with her mother to the supermarket but Debbie and Robert pleaded that they wanted to explore together so, after being warned to behave they found themselves free to do what they liked.

They found a bench on the quayside and Robert pulled the pendant out of his pocket. 'I've cleaned it up a bit,' he said.

Chumley, quiet for once, lay down at Robert's feet, put his head on his paws and watched the boats, the passers-by and the seagulls. Debbie had eyes only for the amazing object nestled in Robert's palm. Despite the smears of dirt and particles of earth still clinging to it, the metal shone and sparkled in the sunlight. The light also picked out three small gems – blue, red and golden yellow.

'It's beautiful!' she said, reaching out to take it carefully from him. 'It's not a pendant, Robert,' she exclaimed in surprise. 'It's a key!'

'Yes I can see that!' retorted Robert. 'The question is

– the key to what? Don't tell me if we dig deeper we'll find a chest full of treasure!'

'You can joke, but we found the note and now we've found this.' Debbie turned the key over thoughtfully, then she looked at Robert, her eyes sparkling. 'I don't think it was an accident us finding the note and the key, Robert.' Even with the sun warm on her back Debbie shivered. 'You know what I think?'

Robert took the key back from Debbie who looked as if she might drop it in her excitement. 'Do I ever?' he replied.

'I think there really is someone called Katherine, who's in danger – and we've been led to this note and key so we can help her.' Debbie paused to see how Robert was reacting to this revelation. Robert was looking down at the key in his hands.

'This key,' he said, 'is the one that someone in the note is after. I think we've got to get it to that girl called Caroline.'

'Katherine,' corrected Debbie automatically. She jumped to her feet. 'Come on, let's go and find her.'

Chumley, who had dozed off, woke with a start and began barking, shattering the peace of the afternoon. A fisherman looked up from the tackle he was mending and glared at them.

Robert smiled at him apologetically, picked up Chumley's lead and followed Debbie.

'Hang on, Debbie. Where exactly are we going?'

Debbie stopped in her tracks and looked at her brother, suddenly downcast. 'I don't know,' she said. 'And I don't know what got into me then either. What a stupid idea!'

'No,' said Robert, considering as Chumley pulled at his lead, eager to be off. 'I think you're right. I don't think it *is* a coincidence finding this stuff. If you're wrong — say it's something buried from a robbery — then we ought to show it to someone. Ask Mum or Dad . . .'

'Or go to the police station,' added Debbie, not liking any of the ideas.

'But first of all we could try and find out something about it. It might be a famous key.'

'We could try the library,' suggested Debbie, brightening up.

'Or the museum,' said Robert thoughtfully. 'They should have some information about the original castle there too.'

'And maybe about Katherine, ' said Debbie, recovering her old excitement.

They passed the library on the way to the museum. It was closed. That was a disappointment. But, to their relief, the museum was open. They tied Chumley up to a bracket meant for bicycles and went inside.

It was a small place, but attractively laid out with several larger exhibits as well as glass cases round the walls. As they went in a grey-haired lady looked at them suspiciously from behind a table near the door. She watched them as they wandered round, looking at the exhibits, growing more and more disappointed.

'There's nothing here,' whispered Robert. 'We'll have to ask *her*.'

Debbie glanced at the lady behind the table and shook her head. 'I'm not asking her anything!'

'Fine lot of help you're going to be, rescuing this Katherine from danger!' Robert sneered. 'I'll ask.'

The grey-haired lady knew nothing, but only because there was nothing to be known. The ruins at Polmar Tor might have been a castle but there was no record of a castle there in the local history of the area. They might be the ruins of a church and the few remaining buildings of a village which had slipped into the sea. Of course they could have dated from any time. It was no use their looking in the library, which was closed anyway, because they wouldn't find any information which she didn't have.

She smiled coldly at Debbie. 'And if that's your dog

barking outside, I wouldn't leave it while you go inside anywhere else. I should take it home,' she said.

Seething with anger, Debbie untied Chumley. 'Shut up!' she said crossly as Chumley barked at a retreating spaniel. Chumley licked her hand and wagged his tail.

'Come on,' said Robert, 'nearly time to meet Mum and Dad. Don't let her upset you, Debbie. In a way, what she said helps.'

Debbie looked at him in surprise as they set off down the street. 'What d'you mean?' she asked intrigued.

'The fact that nobody knows anything about the ruins makes it seem even stranger that we should find what we did,' explained Robert. Debbie looked at him, puzzled. 'I mean if the site is such a mystery, archaeologists would have been buzzing all over it long before this. If there was anything there to find, they would have found it.'

'It doesn't make sense, does it?' said Debbie as they crossed the road.

Ian and Janet Matthews were already waiting outside the café. Chumley went into a frenzy of excitement as he saw them and pulled Debbie along the pavement at such speed that she had no further chance to say anything to Robert. But what else was there to say anyway? If they couldn't even find out who Katherine was what could they possibly do to help her?

Chapter five

The silent figures at the edge of the Far Woods moved apart as a girl's voice cut sharply through the night. 'You stupid idiots, you've knocked him out!'

As the figures separated, Mig could see the still form of Kate lying at their feet. Infuriated, Mig forgot her fears and sprang forward. To her satisfaction the figures fled. Cautiously Mig prodded Kate with a large, velvet paw and gently licked her face. Kate stirred and moaned.

'You cowards!' came the girl's voice shrilly. 'Get that cat!'

Mig stiffened and Kate, clutching her head, struggled to sit up. Three figures edged towards them. Mig attempted a warning roar. The figures froze in their tracks. Pleased with the result, Mig roared again.

Kate moaned. 'Mig, will you stop that. My head aches enough as it is.' She rose shakily to her feet. 'And you . . . you ruffians, keep your distance or . . . my cat will tear you to pieces.' The effect was unnerving: the girl standing erect with her hair streaming out behind her and one hand poised on the sleek coat of the fierce black cat. Then Mig, pleased to have Kate sound her normal self again, spoiled it by purring loudly.

'Mig, for goodness sake!' hissed Kate. Mig came to

her senses and growled again but it was too late for the figures were edging nearer.

The moon, which had disappeared behind the scurrying clouds, broke clear and filtered silver light through the black tracery of the trees. Kate saw the figures of her attackers clearly for the first time and felt a sense of relief. They were not rough, powerful men, but two boys, one of whom was smaller than herself, and a girl with long, black hair, who looked to be her own age. At the same time the other three saw Kate clearly and the taller of the boys let out an exclamation of surprise.

'It's a girl!'

Kate, realising her cap had fallen from her head, saw it lying a few paces away and stooped swiftly to pick it up. 'Keep away from me,' she said warningly, 'or you'll be sorry.'

The girl spoke then and her voice was soothing so that Kate wondered if she had imagined the hardness she had heard in it before. A regretful smile softened her heart-shaped face. 'We are sorry. Please forgive us. We thought that you were a boy.'

Kate touched the back of her head. 'I suppose you think that makes it all right. You knock out any unsuspecting traveller that comes along in anything except a dress! You might have killed me!'

'We might still do,' said the shorter boy, talking for the first time in a gruff voice. 'I don't think we can trust her to go free. I say we get rid of her anyway.'

Kate edged closer to Mig. She looked at the girl who seemed to be more friendly, sorry now that she had spoken abruptly. Even with Mig to help her, the odds were against her. She was no match for three of them and the taller of the two boys looked strong and powerfully built.

'Remember your place, Graf,' the girl said sharply. She turned to Kate. 'Don't worry. We won't hurt you. Go your way in peace.'

Kate swallowed hard and began edging away from the

trio, being careful not to turn her back to the boy called
Graf. A voice stopped her in her tracks. 'Wait!'

Kate hesitated, her heart beating fast. The taller of
the boys was moving towards her. His hazel eyes looked
friendly in the moonlight, but she waited uneasily for
him to speak. 'Are you turning back because you are
afraid to travel alone?' he asked.

She touched her aching head. 'You've hardly given
me any reason to believe it would be safe!' she retorted.

The boy laughed. 'You're right! But we attacked you
only because we feared you might be someone who
would attack us. Travel with us and you will be safe.'

Kate looked at him. His face seemed open and honest
but his eyes sparkled with an expression she could not
read. She studied his companions. Graf was glaring at
them both sullenly. The girl returned her gaze steadily,
then said warmly,' I should be glad of the company of
another girl.' She smiled. 'Even if she is dressed like a
boy!'

Mig moved restlessly at Kate's side. Kate stroked her,
wondering if she could trust this ill-assorted trio. She
glanced at Graf again. The girl followed her gaze. 'Pay
no attention to him. He will do as I say. Won't you,
Graf?'

Graf shrugged and turned away. 'Please yourself!' he
muttered.

'Are you hungry?' the tall boy asked. Mig, at Kate's
side, heard something she could understand at last and
put out a tentative paw to the boy. He laughed and
stroked her head. 'Come and eat with us. We will exchange tales and you can make your decision then. If
you choose to go back to where you have come from I
will bring you back to this same spot and you are free
to go.'

'All right,' Kate said.

'Good,' said the boy. He turned to lead the way deep
into the wood. The girl came to Kate's side and Graf
followed moodily behind. With each step Kate wondered

if she had made the right choice — wondered if she was letting herself be led into a trap.

Chapter six

Robert asked if they could call in at Polmar Tor again on their way home. His father gave him a funny look and said he had planned to call in at another of the churches in his parish.

'Why this interest in Polmar Tor?' Ian Matthews asked.

Debbie gave Robert a warning look.

'It's just that the lady in the museum said nobody knew what the ruins were exactly,' explained Robert, beginning to wish he hadn't brought the subject up.

'That's funny,' said his mother, coming unwittingly to the rescue. 'Barbara Thrower definitely said they were castle ruins. She said we should visit the castle ruins at Polmar Tor because the view was so lovely. You can ask her about it when we go there to tea tomorrow.'

Robert cringed. He did not relish the thought of the Thrower family with the two dreadful girls being the source of their information. As it happened, he and Debbie found out all they wanted to know about the ruins long before they went to the Throwers' house for tea.

When they arrived at the little church they found they needed to get the key from the verger. Robert was sent to knock at the door of his whitewashed cottage. A small man with wispy white hair and a bushy moustache opened the door. His blue eyes twinkled at Robert with lively interest. 'Ah!' he exclaimed when Robert had explained his errand. 'You've come about the key!'

Robert nodded, smiling. He smiled partly in response to the warm smile of the verger, which lifted the ends of his bushy moustache, and partly at his own thoughts. A key was certainly the thing that was on his mind — but not the one the verger meant! So Robert was surprised, as he followed the verger down the leafy pathway through the graveyard to the church, to feel his scalp prickle. Later when the verger invited them all into his cottage for a cup of tea, the feeling grew that he was about to discover something after which things would never be the same.

The verger's cottage was a surprise. The small living-room was crammed with bookcases overflowing with books of all kinds. He left Ian and Janet Matthews browsing through some books about the history of the area and took Robert and Debbie out into the garden to look at his hens.

'You know a lot about places round here?' Robert asked the verger as they walked down the garden path.

The old man turned his lively blue eyes on Robert and Debbie. 'You're wanting to know about the castle on Polmar Tor, I've no doubt, and the mysterious kingdom of Mondar,' he said.

Robert and Debbie turned to each other wide-eyed and surprised at the completely unexpected question.

'Yes,' said Debbie catching her breath, 'we do. We want to know about the castle.'

'And the key?' added Robert, remembering the strange feelings which had begun when the verger had asked him if he'd come about the key.

'Oh yes, the Key of Zorgen,' said the verger, looking at their hopeful faces. He paused as they reached a bench set beneath an old apple tree and eased himself down onto it. 'Then we'd best sit awhile and I'll tell you the whole story.'

Robert sat next to him with Debbie on the warm grass at his feet.

'It's not a story to be taken lightly,' he warned. 'And you won't find anything about it in the history books or museums.'

'Why not?' asked Debbie disappointed. 'Isn't it a true story? You talked about a mysterious kingdom. Isn't it real?'

The verger smiled. 'Well, you're asking some questions there! Is the story I'm going to tell you true? It's legend. That's what I'm going to tell you — the legend of Mondar. But that doesn't mean it isn't true in its own way. Is Mondar real? Best call it a secret place, I fancy.'

The old man leaned back against the trunk of the tree and it seemed to Robert and Debbie as if his gaze travelled beyond the flower-filled garden to scenes in a time long ago.

'Bedien was King of Mondar. He was supposed to look after the Key of Zorgen because the ruler of Mondar had to be the one who had the key. He was a good man but one day when he was away on some business, the Key of Zorgen went missing. Fear was that someone had got hold of it who was not a follower of Zorgen.'

'What happened?' asked Robert anxiously. 'Did they find the key? Did everything turn out all right?'

Robert and Debbie waited with bated breath for his answer. 'Ah,' he said at last, 'that's a difficult one, that is. I don't rightly know the answer. The key hasn't been put into the right hands for the right purpose yet.'

'But,' protested Debbie, 'I thought all this happened a long time ago.'

'In a way yes. In a way no,' said the verger. Mondar is a special kind of place. You must understand that it's very different. You see . . .'

It was at that point, with Robert and Debbie hanging on the verger's every word and the mystery of Mondar and the key about to be explained, that their parents came out into the garden to look for them, because it was time to go.

'Please,' begged Debbie, 'couldn't we stay a few minutes more?'

'I'm afraid not,' said their father firmly.

'Perhaps you'll let the children come again soon?' offered the verger as he saw the look of disappointment which crossed Debbie and Robert's faces.

'That's very kind,' said their mother, looking rather surprised at the friendship that had sprung up so quickly between her children and the old Cornishman.

'Tomorrow?' suggested Debbie hopefully.

'Maybe Monday,' said her mother. 'Don't forget tomorrow we're going out to tea.'

That night Debbie went to bed early, taking with her one of the books on local history which the verger had lent them. She began reading eagerly. Both she and Robert felt sure that what they had found, incredible though it seemed, was the Key of Zorgen. They wished afterwards that they had shown it to the verger and asked him what he thought about it. Debbie also wished she had asked him about Katherine. They still knew nothing about her — except that if she was a princess she might well be the daughter of the king of this place, Mondar. But then again she could just as well be the daughter of another king — perhaps his enemy? Debbie sighed. It was so frustrating. They knew enough to arouse their interest but not enough for them to do anything.

Debbie snapped the book shut. It was no help at all. The verger had been right. There was nothing in it about the castle — except what they knew already from the woman in the museum — and there was certainly nothing about Mondar. She put her light out and tried to settle down to sleep.

It was a warm night and Debbie tossed and turned. She longed for the comforting familiarity of her old room in London. It seemed as if the world was becoming a strange and alien place. For the first time she began to feel vaguely frightened at the idea of the lost kingdom of Mondar, its hidden treasures and a girl called Katherine who was in danger. Despite the heat she pulled the covers up over her head and burrowed into her bed, trying to shut out the disturbing images which filled her mind.

'Debbie!'

She jumped at the sound, no more than a whisper, of a voice calling her name. Then it came again, a second time, more urgently. 'Debbie!'

Cautiously she poked her head over her quilt and switched on her bedside lamp. Robert was peering round her bedroom door.

'Are you awake?' he asked unnecessarily.

He crept into the room and perched himself on the end of Debbie's bed. Debbie could see in the lamplight that his eyes were shining with excitement. By the time he had finished talking Debbie was excited too, all her earlier fears forgotten. It seemed that Robert had been luckier than she in the book which the verger had lent him. His book had contained a section on old Cornish legends, stories and songs.

'And this is the rhyme,' he said, opening the page. It doesn't mention Bedien and I'm afraid there's no mention of any Katherine but . . . well, read it for yourself.'

So Debbie read it. 'Legend attributes this fragment of poetry or song to the area around the ruins of Polmar Tor' was all it said. Three verses were printed.

Let this story be told but not written
Till the time comes to pass when brave men
Know that they need for each thought and deed
Trust in the secret of Zorgen.

Let the castle be ruined and stand empty
And men not understand what they see
Until they add wisdom to courage
And take in both hands Zorgen's key.

Let the lesson be learned by the seekers
That the dark times of peril and war
Can be faced only with Zorgen's son
And the hidden secret of Mondar.

'Oh,' said Debbie disappointed. 'They don't explain what it means.'

'The middle verse, stupid!' said Robert impatiently. 'It's about the castle and the key!'

Debbie read it again. 'Yes, but I still don't see what there is to get so excited about. I can't understand what it means.'

'That's not the point,' interrupted Robert. 'Don't you see what it means for us? This poem's been around for donkey's years and no one else has ever gone to the castle ruins and found the key.'

'Yes. I see what you mean,' said Debbie, her heart beating fast.

'So it's up to us to do something.'

'Do what?'

'I don't know exactly, but I would have thought that we need to go to this Mondar place.'

'Yes,' breathed Debbie. 'We have to take the key to Mondar. But how?'

Robert's idea was to get up just before dawn and cycle to Polmar Tor, which he thought would probably take them about an hour. They would leave a note for their parents to say they had gone out for an early morning bike ride. They had the hazy idea of nipping into Mondar, finding Katherine, giving her the key and getting back before breakfast!

The sky was lightening from a deeper to a paler blue and the stars were beginning to fade when they stole silently out of the house and got their bikes out of the garage. If they had thought about it sensibly in the cold light of day, they would probably not have attempted it, but they could think of nothing except the excitement of being able to do something about the mystery of the key.

They hadn't intended taking Chumley with them but when he saw they meant to steal off somewhere without him, he had begun whining. They had rushed him out of the house before he woke their parents up.

Wisps of lemon and pale pink cloud were touching the horizon as they cycled across the heath towards the tor. Debbie's excitement increased with each passing mile. Soon she might meet the mysterious Katherine.

Chumley was tired by the time they reached the castle ruins. He lay quietly at the foot of the slope while Robert and Debbie nervously performed the ceremony which they hoped would take them into Mondar.

It had been Robert's idea that the key itself would get them into Mondar. Since there was no door into which it could be fitted, perhaps it would be enough if he and Debbie held it in their linked hands. Debbie had added the suggestion that they repeat the rhyme Robert had found while they held the key. Then, for good measure, they decided they would keep their eyes closed until the ceremony was complete.

So, with eyes closed and hands holding the key, they recited together the words of the poem. When it was done Debbie opened her eyes slowly, excited yet fearful of what she would see. She saw Robert standing with his eyes closed in front of her and beyond him, green grass, blue sky — and Chumley sitting at the bottom of the slope.

'You can open your eyes,' she said glumly. 'It hasn't worked.'

They spent a few useless minutes discussing other ways of trying to get into Mondar — doing the same thing with their eyes open; digging for a box — or even a door! — in which to fit the key; coming back at midnight . . . In the end they decided there was nothing they could do except go home and try again after they had seen the verger on Monday.

Chumley, having no disappointment to bear and

having had a good rest, set off for home with a renewed burst of energy. He was far ahead of Debbie and Robert when he came to a wood a short distance from the tor and caught a very interesting scent. He heard Debbie's anxious call as he veered off in the direction of the wood, but the scent was too tantalising to resist.

When Debbie and Robert reached the wood and dismounted from their bikes, Chumley was nowhere in sight. Debbie was angry and near to tears. This move to Cornwall had been a disaster from the start. She was upset about not getting into Mondar. Now Chumley disappearing into this shadowy wood was the last straw. Robert touched her arm. 'You stay here with the bikes. I'll go.'

Debbie attempted a smile. 'We'll go together,' she said.

They propped the bikes up against the tree at the edge of the wood and made their way through the tangle of trees calling, 'Chumley!'

Chumley was actually within earshot but had no intention of turning back for he had caught sight of his quarry. He had never in his life seen anything like it before. It was a cat, as black and as big as Chumley if not bigger. The cat fled and Chumley pursued it, charging through the undergrowth, snapping twigs and sending branches twanging as he went. Then suddenly he lost it. He came to a shuddering halt under a spindly birch.

Behind him Robert and Debbie had also stopped, not knowing which way to turn.

'I'm going back,' said Debbie abruptly. 'There's no sense in us all getting lost.'

Chumley had now picked up a new and enticing scent — the smell of food cooking over an open fire. He rushed forward and, between one tree trunk and the next, stepped into the world which Debbie had longed to find, but from which she was at that moment walking away — the secret kingdom of Mondar.

Chapter seven

Back at the edge of the wood Debbie stopped. She had expected Robert to follow her, but he had not. Now that her anger was cooling she was also beginning to worry about Chumley. She decided to retrace her steps. Brambles caught at her legs as she turned. A low branch scratched her face. But she knew now that she must find Robert and Chumley and get them both safe home. 'Robert, wait! Wait for me!' she called.

Robert was too far into the woods to hear her. He had been tempted to follow Debbie when she had turned and left him, but the thought of Chumley lost and alone, made him press on. He was surprised when, after a few minutes, the darkness of the woods began to lighten and he caught a glimpse of sky and heath. He went eagerly forward only to stop short in amazement at the sight which met his eyes beyond the farthest trees.

Debbie was beginning to wonder if she was going round in circles. There was still no sign of either Robert or Chumley. She no longer knew which way to go. Then a sudden burst of birdsong startled her. Without knowing why she followed the entrancing melody deep into the heart of the wood, calling for Robert and Chumley as she went.

As suddenly as it had begun the birdsong ended, and into the leafy, sun-dappled silence came the sound of her own name. With relief she recognised Robert's voice calling her. 'Debbie! I'm over here.'

She was so glad to see Robert again that at first Debbie did not notice the sight beyond the woods which had set his eyes sparkling with excitement. Then she looked beyond him over the green and gold sea of grass and gorse and her eyes widened in astonished delight.

In front of her stood the towering grey walls of a great castle with yellow and scarlet banners streaming from its turrets. It was surrounded by a wide moat of tranquil water. Debbie looked at Robert with her eyes shining. 'We're in Mondar, aren't we?'

'Looks like we are,' he agreed, grinning.

They started across the heath to the castle, half expecting it to disappear as they got nearer. 'It is real, isn't it?' asked Debbie in quiet tones of awe.

'Real enough, but no good if we can't find a doorway to get in!' Robert replied.

But when they drew nearer to the moat they saw that the drawbridge was down. 'Is it safe, do you think?' asked Debbie.

It had struck them as they had come nearer how quiet everything was. They had seen no one, heard nothing. It was almost as if they were on a stage set, as if nothing else in Mondar was real besides themselves. Much as Debbie had wished herself in Mondar before, now she began to wish herself safely home. She looked at Robert and hesitated, one foot poised to step onto the drawbridge. It was then that she saw, out of the corner of her eye, a shaggy shape come hurtling along from behind Robert, almost knocking her off balance, before charging across the drawbridge and disappearing into the castle courtyard.

'What was that?' exclaimed Robert.

'I think we've found Chumley,' grimaced Debbie, clutching at Robert to stay on her feet, 'and I think we'd better get into that courtyard quickly before we lose him again.'

The courtyard was huge. At its centre was a quiet pool surrounded by a smooth carpet of green lawn. Everywhere were trees, bushes of azaleas and hydrangeas and clumps of bright, summer flowers. At first glance it seemed Chumley had vanished again then Robert saw him cowering under a stone bench amid the scarlet of azalea bushes. He was shivering with fright.

'Hey, old fella, what's happened to you?' asked Robert gently, bending down to stroke him. 'We're here. It's all right now.' But Debbie, looking up at the grey castle walls towering above them, from which windows like empty eyes stared blankly down, wondered if Chumley had already tasted what she and Robert had not — the danger which lay in wait for them in Mondar.

'Excuse me,' said a voice from behind them, 'May I be of any assistance?'

All three turned, startled, to see a girl step out of the shade of a leafy palm tree. She wore a long dress of pale blue, with a ribbon of the same shade laced through her golden hair. She waited politely for a reply. Debbie saw that it was up to her to say something, for Robert, standing wide-eyed and open-mouthed, looked incapable of saying anything. But she hardly knew where to begin for surely, here at last, was Katherine.

Before she could put her thoughts into words, the girl spoke again, lifting dark eyebrows enquiringly. 'Did you wish to see the king?'

'Yes,' said Debbie eagerly, finding her tongue. 'Y . . . yes. King Bedien.'

'He is not here.' She smiled apologetically. 'But I will take you to see Edric, the Chief Steward.'

The girl moved gracefully ahead, leading them into the great hall of the castle. They followed her up the wide staircase and along panelled corridors hung with fine tapestries and decorated with rich carving. Debbie quickened her pace, eager to tell her about the key and the note which warned of danger before they met Edric.

'There's something I need to talk to you about,' she said. 'It's very important.'

The girl turned. 'Yes?' she prompted, smiling.

But Debbie got no further for at that moment there was the loud noise of a crash from a room behind them down the corridor. With a startled look the girl pushed past her and turned into a room on the right, the door of which now stood wide open.

Even before she looked into the room Debbie knew, with a feeling of dread, what she would see. It was a magnificent room dominated by a four poster bed, but Debbie saw only the large shaggy dog sitting trembling in the middle of a heap of disjointed armour. Behind him was the empty stand on which the armour must have hung and between his paws was a belt of linked, silver chains.

'Chumley!' said Debbie sternly. 'Bad dog!' She turned to the girl in dismay and saw that her violet eyes were fixed icily on Chumley. Surely this was the moment to tell her everything, so that instead of being angry she would be grateful and pleased.

'I'm so sorry,' she began. 'But if I could explain . . .'

'Leave it,' the girl said sharply. Debbie stopped in mid-sentence and realised the girl had not heard her. She was watching Robert who had bent to retrieve the fallen armour. Robert kept his hand on the belt that he was trying to prise from Chumley. Chumley growled.

'Please,' said Debbie, desperately to the girl. 'You must listen.'

'Only,' said the girl frostily, 'if you can explain why your animal has behaved so badly.'

Debbie was slightly taken aback. This was not how she had pictured the long-awaited meeting with Katherine. But then if Chumley had damaged her father's armour, Debbie supposed she had every right to be angry.

'Well,' Debbie began, 'it all started when . . .'

'No!' yelled Robert suddenly. 'Debbie, wait!'

Both girls looked at Robert, startled. Robert in turn looked at the belt in his hand and back at the girls in alarm. His face was getting redder by the minute and his glasses were steaming up as he began to gabble an apology. 'I mean, we're very sorry and we'll take Chumley away right now, won't we, Debbie? And we hope the armour is all right and . . . er . . . everything.'

Debbie looked at him, puzzled, as he pulled Chumley away from the armour and towards the door. 'Come on, Debbie,' he muttered, 'we've caused enough trouble.' This behaviour was so unlike Robert that Debbie's confusion only grew. She didn't know if she should follow him or pour the whole story out to the girl. Then the decision was taken out of her hands for, as Robert backed out of the door, he collided with a man who was sharp-featured and imperious.

'And what is going on here?' asked the man.

'Oh, Edric,' said the girl, 'I'm glad you've come.'

Debbie's heart sank. She did not like the look of Edric. His name had stirred a faint feeling of alarm in her the first time the girl had mentioned it. Where had she heard it before? Wherever it was she was sure now that she had been right to want a chance to talk to Katherine alone.

The sharp eyes fell on the scattered suit of armour. 'King Bedien's armour!' he exclaimed angrily. 'It seems I come too late, Marise!'

For a second or two the room swam and Debbie felt dizzy with shock. Not Katherine but Marise! Edric and Marise! She remembered now where she had come across his name before. In the note! She could not recall the exact words but she knew that Marise was not someone Katherine could call a friend . . . and Debbie had been about to tell her about the key!

Edric walked across the room to examine the scattered armour and Marise, with an icy glance at Robert and Debbie, followed him. At the same moment Chumley pulled free of Robert and raced off down the corridor. Robert, trying to grasp the improvised lead, chased after him. Edric and Marise turned at the sound and Debbie had only moments to follow before Marise was after her. She gained a few seconds by overturning a chair in Marise's path but by then Robert and Chumley had rounded a corner and were out of sight. The corridor into which she turned was empty and behind her came the sound of footsteps. Desperately Debbie ran on.

'Debbie, quick. Here!' a voice called softly and a hand reached out and pulled her through a concealed doorway. She fell backwards into darkness. Robert's hand clamped over her mouth to stop her crying out. She could hear Chumley's muffled panting. 'Shh!' said Robert. 'It's all right.'

The footsteps ran past. Robert removed his hand, leaving Debbie gasping. 'Quick,' he said before she had a chance to get her breath back. 'Let's cut back the way we came and get out of here.'

There were people about now. They heard voices and footsteps everywhere as they retraced their steps along the corridor, back to the doorway that led into the court-yard. They moved round the edge of the courtyard, keeping to the shadows where they could. They did not have to go as far as the drawbridge for they found a gateway which led outside. Once on the headland there was no cover so they ran as fast as they could until they reached the woods.

They sat for a while on a fallen log so that Robert could get his breath back. Debbie wanted to know exactly what had happened to him before she even thought about what they would do next. When he was able to talk she listened in amazement.

'I knew she wasn't to be trusted,' he said, unfastening the lead from Chumley's collar. 'It was the belt.' When Debbie looked at the 'lead' she saw that it was the belt of King Bedien's armour.

'The belt?' she asked.

'Yes. When you touch it, it tells you things.'

Debbie put out a tentative hand. It felt like cool metal but nothing more.

'It's true!' said Robert. 'When I touched it I could see that girl as she really was — not beautiful and friendly but mean and nasty.' He shuddered. 'And then I saw the opening, the one we hid in. Holding the belt I knew it would be safe to hide there. I knew too where it was safe to go till we got clear of the castle.'

'And now?' asked Debbie. 'Does it tell us what to do now?'

'No,' said Robert, struggling to explain. 'It's not like that. It doesn't tell you what to do. It's more that it shows you what's right.'

'Oh,' said Debbie, frowning as she fingered the belt. 'I see.'

Robert laughed as he took the belt from her. 'No. You don't,' he said.

'Shh!' said Debbie, rising to her feet. 'Listen.' She had caught the sound of birdsong once again. 'Can you hear that bird singing? That's the one that led me to you.'

Robert strained to listen. 'How d'you know it's the same bird?'

Debbie reached out and touched the belt. 'It's the same one. I know it is.'

Robert nodded. 'Well, what do we do then?'

'Follow the sound of its singing,' said Debbie, moving forward.

Robert rose reluctantly to his feet. He looked uneasily over his shoulder towards the castle. 'This Mondar, it's a strange place, isn't it?' But Debbie had moved away, entranced by the birdsong.

'They have gone to the Far Woods,' said Edric.

Marise said nothing. She had let the strangers slip out of her hands. Edric had not said anything, but that made her fear his anger even more. Edric laughed and the sound sent a shiver of fear through her. 'Do not worry, my fair Marise,' he said. 'Remember that if they find Katherine, they will also find someone with her who serves Dolan.'

Chapter eight

Kate and her new-found friends left the Far Woods and struck out south-east. They had discovered over a supper shared round their camp fire that each of them was looking for King Bedien. Kate was surprised to learn that the other three had not been long together — only a day or so. They had met by chance in the woods and, finding that they shared the same goal, had decided that they would travel together. Now they were happy for Kate and Mig to travel with them, especially since Mig had chased off a large, hairy dog that had broken into their camp as they were cooking a hurried breakfast.

Walking beside Gerrard, with Mig racing ahead through the long grasses and bracken, Kate had time to think over what the others had told her — which was not really very much. Although they had seemed open and friendly, with even the surly boy, Graf, beginning to accept her, Kate felt there was something they were holding back. But then so was she, for she had no intention of telling three strangers that she was the daughter of the king they each wanted to find.

'Why are you looking for Bedien?' Gerrard asked suddenly.

Kate jumped. It was almost as if he had read her

thoughts. For a minute, looking into his warm, hazel eyes, she was tempted to tell him. Then she remembered how, when she had come to the wood looking for Fleet, she had been attacked instead by Gerrard and Graf.

'I can't tell you,' she said at last.

'All right,' said Gerrard with a wry smile. 'Maybe you can tell me later. You can trust me, you know, Kate.'

Kate looked back over her shoulder at Graf walking beside Astelle. 'Maybe,' she said.

The countryside had begun to change dramatically by the time they stopped to eat lunch. Heathland had given way to moorland. They found a spot where a small stream sparkled in the sunshine, threading its way round boulders, past clumps of heather and fern. The provisions, which the others had been sharing, had been used up with breakfast that morning, so now they ate the last of the bread Kate had brought from the castle with slices of the spiced meat which Kate had imagined would last her several days. There were only three pieces of fruit left — two apples and a pear. Though Gerrard protested that he did not want any, Kate cut them up, dividing them equally between the four of them. She felt a twinge of anxiety at the thought that there was now no food left. It seemed they were miles from anywhere and they would need to reach somewhere where they could buy food before they could eat again.

The countryside stretched away on all sides around them, monotonously the same as they walked on. Kate reminded herself that Gerrard, who seemed to have taken on the role of leader quite naturally, had assured them all that he knew where they were going. Then, as they crossed the brow of a hill, Kate's heart lifted, for ahead of them lay a valley bordered with snowcapped mountains. Somewhere beyond them was the Palace of Pererin. There she would find her father and all her worries about Edric and her present travelling companions would be over.

It was as they crossed the open hill-top, exposed to

mile upon mile of empty moorland behind them, that Kate had an uneasy feeling that she was being watched. Gerrard was walking ahead now with Astelle. Suddenly, at the far edge of the hill, they stopped and, as they turned to look at her, Kate saw their faces were twin pictures of dismay. Kate's heart leapt to her mouth. 'What is it?' she asked, hurrying forward.

Kate had heard her father describe this route and she had studied it on a map, but she had not travelled it since she was a small child. From one foothill to the other, stretching across the entire neck of the valley, was a lake. She stared at it in disbelief.

'There must be some way over it or around it,' said Gerrard, pacing back and forth, examining the wide expanse of water. 'Otherwise how do the villagers get out of this valley?'

'Boats,' said Graf briefly and pointed.

Looking across to the far side of the lake, they saw a landing stage with a dozen or so small boats moored to it.

'But none on this side,' said Kate glumly.

'Don't worry. Zorgen will help us,' said Gerrard confidently. 'Come on, Graf. Let's go down and take a closer look.'

Mig seemed to think herself included in the invitation and set off enthusiastically with Gerrard and Graf. Kate was about to follow when Astelle took her arm.

'Kate,' she said quietly, 'I must talk to you. There is a way to cross the lake.'

'I'll call the boys back,' said Kate moving forward.

'No,' said Astelle urgently, her dark eyes clouding. 'Gerrard mustn't know. It would be too dangerous. You see, there is a monster.'

Kate studied the small face for some sign that she was teasing but Astelle was completely serious.

'A monster!' exclaimed Kate.

'Yes. Shh!' insisted Astelle, drawing Kate away from the hilltop. 'Under the lake is a cavern which is guarded by a terrible monster, a sea-serpent with scales like steel and poisonous fangs. If only one of us could cross the lake through the cavern we could bring back a boat.'

Kate shuddered. 'Why don't we tell the boys?' she asked.

'Because Gerrard would insist on going. He would try to fight the serpent, believing Zorgen would protect him.'

'You don't think Zorgen would?'

Astelle studied Kate for a moment before answering. 'I have never seen Zorgen, Kate. Have you? I would not like to trust someone I could not see, someone I could not be sure was there to help me when my life was in the gravest peril.'

'No,' said Kate, thinking of how, for all her father's talk of Zorgen, danger threatened his daughter the minute he left her alone. And, before that, many years ago when her mother was dying, Zorgen had not healed her. What proof had she that Zorgen would help anyone — if indeed Zorgen existed at all?

'You're right,' she said slowly. 'We can't let Gerrard risk his life. What shall we do, then?' She was afraid that she already knew the answer.

'*We* must go,' Astelle said. 'I have heard it said that the sea-serpent will become powerless if it can be lured away from the treasure it guards. We will draw it away from its treasure, then we will steal past it and fetch the boat.'

She spoke calmly enough but her eyes were bright with an expression that made Kate feel uneasy. Then, as Kate looked deep into her eyes, she began to feel that it was really the only possible solution — to go into the cavern and cross under the lake. Kate felt a strange sensation, as if the sounds and scents of the summer afternoon were fading away and she was becoming locked in a shadowy stillness which drew her to the cavern where the dreadful monster lay.

It was the sudden noise — a series of sharp, short

sounds, that brought her back to reality with a start. Turning her head she saw the large, shaggy animal which, earlier that day had attacked their camp. It was bounding across the moorland straight towards her. She gave a cry of alarm and gripped Astelle's arm.

Astelle shook her free impatiently. 'It's only a dog,' she said and, picking up a large stone, she hurled it at the approaching animal. 'Go away!' she yelled.

The dog stopped in its tracks, whining, then it turned and ran back to the small figure that had appeared over the horizon. Behind Kate the boys were clambering quickly back up the slope.

'What's happening?' asked Gerrard.

'It's a girl and a dog,' said Astelle coolly.

Kate could see now that with the animal there came a girl, dressed as Kate was, like a boy but with strange, close-fitting trousers in a dark shade of blue. Her brown hair was caught up high in some kind of band so that as she hurried forward it swung back and forwards behind her. As she came closer Kate could see that she was angry. She also saw behind the girl, another small figure coming over the horizon.

'Right!' the girl said, glaring at them, 'Which of you lot threw the stone at my dog?'

Kate looked at the large animal which had bared its teeth in a growl. She took a step backwards behind Gerrard. 'Mig!' she called urgently. 'Mig!'

'Oh! You was it!' exclaimed the girl, angrily advancing on Kate.

At that moment Mig, having caught an interesting scent, came flying over the brow of the hill. Chumley, recognising her, retreated behind Debbie and Debbie herself stopped short in alarm. Mig, sensing victory, moved in on her victim, hissing and flexing her claws.

'Mig, stay!' commanded Kate. Mig pretended not to hear till a sharp whack on her rump brought her to a sudden halt. She turned and looked accusingly at Kate.

The anger which had carried Debbie recklessly into

the middle of this group of strangers, had now been replaced by fear. It was eased a little when the big cat had been called off. She was also slightly reassured to find that the strangers were children around her own age. But apart from that they looked a threatening group. The girl with red hair, who Debbie suspected had thrown the stone at Chumley, looked fierce. The other girl stood cool and aloof, her eyes glinting with an expression which made Debbie shiver. The smaller of the boys glowered at her from under dark brows. But it was the tall boy who made her most uneasy — not just because he looked big and strong, but because he was looking at her as if he could see right into her mind; as if he were considering what should be done with her.

As Debbie studied the group, Kate studied Debbie. She saw that the girl's stormy anger had died suddenly and that the sight of Mig had shaken her. Who was she, Kate wondered — someone sent by Marise to follow her? If so, she was a strange choice and her behaviour was even stranger.

Then Kate's attention was drawn away from her as the second figure came closer into view. It was a boy of about the same height as Graf but whereas Graf was thin, he was plump and red-faced with strange glass circles suspended before his eyes. Kate looked at him curiously.

'We mean you no harm,' said Gerrard to the girl. 'In Zorgen's name let there be peace between us.'

Kate looked at him in surprise. She had expected him to ask the girl who she was and where she had come from, wearing such strange clothes.

The girl's face changed at Gerrard's words. 'OK,' she said, and smiled back.

The boy arrived hot and panting. Gerrard offered him one of the flasks of freshly filled water.

'This is my brother, Robert,' the girl explained. 'I'm Debbie and this is our dog, Chumley.'

Gerrard introduced himself. 'You're not from the

village, are you?' he asked.

'The village?' Debbie tried to think quickly. She felt differently about the group now that Gerrard had mentioned the name Zorgen but she still hardly knew anything about them. She certainly was not ready to tell him where she actually did come from. 'No,' she said brightly, 'We're strangers in these parts.'

The girl with dark hair and the boy still had not said anything. Debbie glanced at the girl. The expression in her eyes now was one of friendly interest. Debbie no longer thought her aloof. She was really quite pretty. She reminded Debbie of someone — a pop star perhaps, or someone she had seen on television? Gerrard followed her gaze. 'This is Astelle,' he said. 'And Graf,' he continued, indicating the smaller boy. 'And Mig,' he added, pointing to the large, black cat edging nearer to Chumley, 'who belongs to Kate.' He turned to smile at Kate but, to his surprise, she was no longer there. 'Where's Kate?' he asked.

Debbie had noticed the girl with red hair disappearing into the hillside below them on the left flank of the lake. 'She went into that hill,' she said, pointing. She was beginning to feel that the further they travelled into Mondar, the stranger it seemed.

Gerrard was already striding quickly down the slope towards the hill. Graf followed. The girl called Astelle with the lovely face and the long, smooth curtain of dark hair looked at Debbie for a long moment, a strange expression in her eyes, before she turned on her heels and went after the boys. Chumley was already chasing down the slope after Mig. Debbie raised her eyebrows at Robert and shrugged her shoulders. 'Let's go with them, shall we?'

'You don't think it might be a trap?' asked Robert.

'No,' replied Debbie without hesitation. 'That boy called Gerrard mentioned Zorgen — and I think,' she added, her eyes sparkling, 'that girl with the long, black hair might be Katherine.'

'But she's called Astelle,' protested Robert, scrambling down the slope after her.

'She's in disguise, of course,' said Debbie with exaggerated patience.

'Well,' mumbled Robert, 'I think it's more likely to be the one called Kate. Kate's short for Katherine.'

But Debbie didn't hear, for she had reached the hill and was following the others into an opening which led into a dank, dark tunnel. 'Come on, Robert,' she called and her voice echoed eerily back.

Another voice from in front of her said sharply, 'Quiet! We don't know what's ahead of us in there.'

The ground underfoot was squelchy and uneven. Debbie put one foot carefully in front of the other. By the flickering flame of a tallow torch held high in someone's hand, she could see the shape of the winding tunnel sloping steeply downward and the shadowy forms of the others moving on ahead. The tunnel seemed to slope for ever, curving to the right. Shadows leapt at her from the walls as she moved fearfully forward. She actually found herself longing for the comfort and safety of the new house in Polmar.

Because her thoughts were far away it was a greater shock when suddenly she came upon an unexpected sight round the next corner. The tunnel had opened out into a vast cavern. The light of the torch in Gerrard's hands showed them only part of it. The rest was lost in grotesque shadows. She could see plainly a mound of treasure gleaming in the darkness and, next to it, something which made her gasp with horror. Uncoiling itself from the dank ground was a huge, monstrous shape. Debbie had never seen anything like it. The sight of its great, heavy scales slinking forward filled her with fear. The huge jaws with the darting red tongue opened and its cold, yellow eyes looked from one to the other of the children, passing over Debbie and finally settling on Kate, standing in the centre of the cavern.

Debbie saw, with some small sense of relief, that the

64

serpent could not reach Kate because a wide chasm separated the main part of the cavern from the part where they stood near the tunnel mouth. But her relief was short-lived for she saw now what Kate was doing. She was winding up a bridge which was suspended over the side of the chasm and which, when it was pulled up to stretch out on a level, would reach across to the other side.

Chapter nine

Robert's journey along the tunnel had been a difficult one. He was so far behind Debbie that the torchlight, which just about showed the way for her, barely reached him. He had the added problem that Mig and Chumley, who had entered the tunnel behind him, kept scampering ahead, then turning back so that he was never sure when he might trip over a large, furry animal. In the end he managed to grab Chumley in passing and attached King Bedien's belt to his collar again.

His feeling of relief as he stepped into the cavern and saw the others was quickly replaced by horror. He saw the serpent on the far side of the chasm and Kate pulling up the bridge. The belt in his hand showed him something which none of the others could see — an aura of evil hanging round the sea-serpent like a thick cloud of sulphur. Then out of the corner of his eye he saw the same awful cloud on this side of the cavern and, turning his head quickly, glimpsed it around Astelle. But he could not be sure for in that instant, as he turned, Chumley broke free and the belt was torn out of his grasp. He saw only Astelle, pale and lovely, looking anxiously at Kate.

Chumley had been growling fiercely from the minute

he had seen the sea-serpent. Now he ran towards the chasm, barking ferociously. Robert was afraid he had not seen the chasm and was about to rush headlong over the edge. 'Chumley!' he yelled.

Kate, gripped by the need to lure the serpent away from the treasure, had been completely unaware of anything else until she heard Robert's cry. She turned to see Chumley rushing towards the chasm and lunged quickly sideways to grab his lead. Chumley skidded to a halt, inches from the edge. Kate had only a moment to feel relieved before she saw a new danger.

Across the chasm the serpent was slithering towards the bridge which was now almost level with the far bank. She realised as she saw the murderous gleam in his yellow eyes that his evil power was far stronger than she had imagined. Merely getting him further away from the treasure was not going to affect him at all. If he crossed the chasm they were all in great danger. She released the belt attached to Chumley's collar and moved quickly to unwind the bridge and drop it back into the chasm's side. Strangely, as she moved forward, the sea-serpent seemed less menacing. It retreated to the shadows on the side of the cavern away from the treasure. Kate was tempted to think that what she had seen a moment ago was a trick of the imagination. She paused, her hand on the pulley which controlled the bridge.

The decision of what to do next was taken out of Kate's hands, for Mig, who decided to demonstrate her courage now that the serpent was retreating, ran onto the bridge and leapt the short gap onto the other side. It seemed to Kate that she had no choice but to follow Mig to get her back. She was on the bridge and crossing it before she had time to think of the danger, then hesitating only a second, she jumped the gap. Gerrard, pulling a sharp dagger from beneath his tunic, ran quickly onto the bridge after her, with Graf at his heels. Debbie would have followed but Astelle took her arm and stopped her.

Robert moved to the edge of the chasm where Chumley sat, still shivering from fright. With one hand he stroked the large, shaggy head reassuringly while with the other he reluctantly took up the lead, half afraid of what the belt might show him on the far side of the cavern.

He saw the sea-serpent coiled once again in the centre of the foul cloud of sulphur and he shuddered at the cunning in its slitted, yellow eyes. He sensed that it was waiting and he saw its eyes were fixed on Kate.

Caught on the edge of the cloud, he saw Graf stealing towards the treasure and reaching out his hand towards a bag of gold. The sea-serpent took no notice of the thief. He was slowly unwinding his sinewy scales. Robert knew that at any minute he would strike out at Kate and that Gerrard, with his small dagger, would be no match for him. Now Gerrard was between Kate and the serpent, telling her to get Mig safely back across the bridge. Kate hesitated and Robert rose to his feet in alarm for he could see that the serpent was seconds away from striking.

In that critical moment of danger, Robert's attention was caught by something shining in the heap of treasure at the other side of the cavern. Without understanding how it could help, he yelled to Kate, 'Kate, get that silver thing out of the treasure. Give it to Gerrard. Quick!'

Incredibly, Kate, who had seemed to be in a trance, heard and understood him. She moved quickly to the heap of treasure and pulled out a slightly curved rectangle of metal. Robert could now see it was a a piece of armour, a breastplate, he thought. In the same moment that Kate moved away from Gerrard's protection, the sea-serpent rose menacingly and opened its huge mouth. Kate stood paralysed with fear as the poisonous tongue darted out at her.

'In the name of Zorgen, hold!' cried Gerrard, moving with lightning speed to Kate's side and lifting the hand in which she held the breastplate so that, at the last moment, it came between Kate and the sea-serpent's lethal tongue.

Robert's eyes widened to see the cloud of sulphur swell and writhe and the fury of the serpent at its centre grow even greater. But it did nothing. It was as if the breastplate was a shield which protected Kate and Gerrard from its murderous fangs.

Holding the breastplate in front of him and with Kate behind him, Gerrard edged back towards the bridge. Mig needed no encouragement to scurry ahead of Kate and leap onto the bridge. The wooden planks of the bridge gave a little beneath her weight and Mig had to dig her claws in and scramble frantically to cross the bridge, now sloping downwards towards the chasm. Kate, looking back over her shoulder, gasped in alarm as she saw the wide gap and the precarious foothold which the bridge now offered.

'Come on, Kate, jump,' cried Astelle, running forward. She and Graf, who had recrossed earlier, leaned dangerously near the edge of the chasm, ready to offer hands to catch her if she slipped. Debbie tried to move the pulley to rewind the bridge but, to her dismay, the mechanism had jammed. She felt it jolt in her hands as Kate landed heavily on the bridge. Debbie looked up and, to her horror, saw Kate slipping backwards out of reach of Astelle and Graf's outstretched hands. Then, to Debbie's relief, she gained a hold and slowly pulled herself forward till Astelle and Graf were able to haul her to safety.

The relief of having Kate safely across was quickly replaced by concern for Gerrard. Thanks to the jammed mechanism, the bridge had not dropped much under Kate's landing but it was difficult to see how Gerrard, holding dagger and breastplate, could possibly catch hold of the bridge. It seemed to be only the breastplate between him and sure death from the serpent's fangs. He could not let it go before he was out of the serpent's reach. Standing at the edge of the chasm, Gerrard looked behind him and saw for the first time the predicament he was in. Immediately he dropped his dagger. The others watched it spiraling downwards into bottomless darkness. Debbie thought of Gerrard following his dagger and felt sick with fear.

She gasped as she saw Gerrard leaping for the bridge and gaining only the slenderest hold with his free hand. His legs dangled over the edge of the bridge, pulling him backwards.

'Let go the breastplate,' yelled Kate.

At the same time a sudden sense of urgency made Robert unhook the belt from Chumley's collar. It also made him do something which looked unwise for such a plump boy. He stretched out along the bridge as far as it seemed safe, then he snaked the belt out in front of him until it was level with Gerrard's hand. He saw to his alarm the whitening of Gerrard's knuckles and knew he could not hold on much longer. 'Gerrard, try and grab the belt,' he gasped.

As soon as she realised what Robert was doing, Debbie rushed forward. 'Help me,' she called desperately to the others. They hurried to her side and, lying flat on the ground at the edge of the bridge, took hold of Robert's legs. They all held on with every ounce of their strength, but even so they felt themselves pulled forwards as the weight increased almost unbearably, telling them that Gerrard had managed to release his hold on the bridge and grasp the belt. They pulled and felt their heavy burden move very slightly forward.

Debbie felt the strength draining from her hands and knew she would not be able to hold on any longer. In desperation she recalled the one thing that had helped before. Gerrard had called on Zorgen. 'Help, Zorgen, please,' she whispered between gritted teeth. In that moment her hold on Robert slipped completely, but at the same time she felt a hot breath on her cheek and the brush of soft fur against her arm. She heard Kate's weak cry of relief. 'Mig's got him.'

Looking up Debbie saw Robert struggling to his feet and Mig on the bridge, pulling between her strong teeth the belt to which Gerrard was clinging desperately. The bridge began to dip down more steeply but Mig was moving rapidly and easily backwards till she had Gerrard almost to the bank where they could pull him to safety with eager hands. The belt, released from Mig's clenched teeth, plummeted to the depths of the chasm. Seconds later the bridge finally gave way.

Relief washed over the exhausted children as they looked across the chasm at the serpent, now powerless to harm them. Then Astelle, standing at the edge of the group, gave a cry of alarm. 'Look!' she jerked out, pointing at the serpent with a trembling hand.

The serpent was changing before their eyes. It reared itself on short, scaly legs and strode to the edge of the chasm. Its eyes, now burning with cold fires of hate, scanned the six children. Then it opened its mouth, belching out blue flame which blazed across the stony earth at their feet. Debbie, standing next to Astelle, clutched her arm. The cavern on their side of the chasm was being transformed into a winter nightmare of treacherous ice at their feet and sharp pellets of crystal, raining like hailstones down on their heads. A damp, white mist swirled around them, chilling them to the bone.

Gerrard, still weak and shaken, staggered to his feet. 'Let's get out of here!' he cried.

They needed no second urging. With Graf leading the way with the torch, they all headed as quickly as they dared for the tunnel. The ground underfoot was now very slippery, the air thick with crystals, shot through with particles of blue and silver ice.

Debbie was almost numb with cold when she glimpsed the tunnel mouth ahead at last. She could make out the shadowy shapes of the others huddled together where the mists thinned. Then, drawing level with them, she saw a sight which chilled her more deeply than the freezing blizzard blowing around her. Stars shone in a bright sky and under them stretched a bleak and alien landscape. The summer world which they had left outside the tunnel was no longer there. Behind them blew the blizzard and in front of them stretched a limitless expanse of ice and snow.

Chapter ten

Debbie looked around her with a sinking heart. 'What's happened?' she asked, her teeth chattering with cold. She wished even more than before that she was back in her room in Polmar.

'I don't know,' said Gerrard coming up to her and putting his arm around her shoulders. 'But don't worry, Debbie. The power of that sea-serpent isn't greater than the power of Zorgen. What the serpent means for ill Zorgen can use for good.' Then he turned to the others, rubbing his arms to bring back feeling into them. 'Come on. We must keep moving. We have a journey to make and Zorgen will help us.'

Kate came forward then, leaving Mig, who had huddled next to Chumley for warmth. 'Gerrard is right,' she said. 'If we stay here we will die from the cold.' She stepped out in the direction of the lake, leaving the others to follow.

Once on the move, Debbie discovered that the feeling came back to her frozen limbs. The air was crisp and clear and it was better than the stinging mist and hail of the cavern. She walked behind Robert and Gerrard and could overhear snatches of their conversation. Robert was telling Gerrard about the belt and Gerrard in turn was saying how he had felt that he had to hang onto the breastplate. He told him how Zorgen, the great Maker and Keeper of Mondar and the world beyond, helped him in knowing what to do. Debbie quickened her steps to catch them up.

'Do you think that Zorgen could do the same for Debbie and me, even though we don't know him?' Robert was asking as Debbie drew alongside.

Debbie caught her breath, not sure what Gerrard's answer would be. Not sure even if Gerrard would understand what Robert meant. She knew that Robert was asking not just about what was happening to them now. He was wondering if Zorgen could touch their lives back in the world they had come from. Was it Zorgen who had led them to find the key? Zorgen who had brought them into Mondar on this strange and dangerous mission?

Gerrard did not reply. He looked first at Robert and then at Debbie. She could not read the expression in his hazel eyes as she waited for his answer. She wanted very much to be told that Zorgen was interested not just in Gerrard but in herself and Robert as well.

Gerrard's face broke into a smile. Debbie let her breath out in a long sigh of relief. Somehow the smile gave her the answer she wanted to hear even before Gerrard put it into words. 'Yes. Zorgen can do everything for you that he does for me. But I think you probably know him — at least a little — in your own world.'

Such was Debbie and Robert's delight in hearing this news it took a second or two longer before they realised what else Gerrard had said: 'In your own world.'

Robert looked quickly over his shoulder to make sure that Graf and Astelle, who were trudging along a little distance behind them, were out of earshot before he dropped his voice, 'You know we come from another world?'

'So it's true!' said Gerrard softly, his breath misting

in the frosty air. He shook his head as if the slight motion would clear his thoughts. 'I didn't know. I just felt it.' He gave a low laugh. 'But to hear you say it, Robert — it gives me the same kind of feeling that the bridge giving way under me did just now!'

They continued walking for a few minutes through the still, white world in silence. There was so much to think about in the discoveries they had just made. So many questions to ask. So much to tell each other. It was hard to know where to begin.

'Tell him about the key, Robert,' whispered Debbie.

'You tell him about the note first,' returned Robert.

'All right,' Debbie agreed, seeing the sense in his suggestion. It would be a relief to pour out the whole story to someone; to have someone like Gerrard help them know what to do.

But, for better or worse, the opportunity for sharing their story slipped out of their hands before Debbie had time to say anything. While she and Robert had been talking Gerrard had walked a short distance ahead to catch up with Kate. Now they came to a sudden halt at the top of a hill. Gerrard let out a shout of delight.

'Look at the lake!' he cried.

Debbie came up to his side and everything else was forgotten as she caught her breath in wonder at the enchanting beauty of the snow-covered valley in the starlight. At their feet the impassable lake was now a sheet of frozen ice. Gerrard's words of a few moments before came back to her: 'What the serpent means for ill Zorgen can use for good.' Was this Zorgen's work, turning what had seemed a disaster into the answer to their problem?

'What is it?' asked Astelle eagerly, coming to stand between Debbie and Gerrard. 'What's happened to the lake?'

Robert, bursting with excitement, turned to answer her. He thought he glimpsed a look of dismay in Astelle's dark eyes as she caught sight of the ice-covered lake. Perhaps she had not understood what it meant.

'We can cross it!' he announced enthusiastically.

'If it takes our weight,' said Graf doubtfully.

'There's only one way to find out,' exclaimed Kate, glaring at him. With Mig following in a flurry of snow, she slithered down the hill. She had reached the lake and stepped onto it before anyone could stop her.

'Kate! Be careful!' yelled Gerrard. Even as he spoke Kate lost her footing, screamed and landed with a thump on the ice. Gerrard let out a roar of laughter and Kate, getting gingerly to her feet, yelled at him crossly. 'Well, you see if you can do better!'

'If only we had some skates,' Debbie said to Robert.

Gerrard had now joined Kate on the lake and, as he stepped on, to Debbie's amazement and Kate's annoyance, he moved effortlessly over the frozen surface as if he wore the finest skates.

The others clambered down eagerly to the lakeside to enjoy Gerrard's skating display. Even Kate smiled as he performed a graceful figure of eight and came to a halt with an elaborate bow. They all laughed as Mig, seeing how easily he moved, attempted to reach Kate and went sprawling, all four paws splayed out as she spun round in a circle.

'All very well, Master Ice-Expert,' said Kate, helping a stunned Mig to her feet. 'But we can't all cross the lake wearing whatever it is you've got on your feet — which I think, without any offence to your natural skill, is the only reason you haven't fallen flat on your face.'

They all looked down at Gerrard's feet and saw that he was wearing not skates but a pair of soft boots which gleamed silver like the stars overhead against the brightness of the ice.

Gerrard shrugged his shoulders and arched an eyebrow to show his own surprise. They could see it was an effort for him to keep still and not let the wonderful boots take him on their dancing journey. 'I don't know how I got them, Kate,' he said, smiling, 'but they make me feel wonderful. I feel now that everything is going to be all right. Things are going to work out, Kate.'

'Fine,' said Kate impatiently, wincing as Mig rubbed against one of her many bruises, 'but we haven't *all* got marvellous new boots. How are the rest of us going to get across?'

Debbie could see that Kate had a point. She could also see that Kate was still annoyed about her fall and that if Gerrard didn't come up with a good idea quickly, things could become rather unpleasant. Much to her surprise it was Robert who came to the rescue.

'I've got an idea,' he exclaimed excitedly. 'I'm not sure if it will work but it's worth a try.'

The others were not very enthusiastic when Robert explained what he meant. But, since no one had a better idea, they were all willing to try it — except for Graf who thought Gerrard should cross alone. 'Stupid idea,' he muttered.

To Robert's surprise, it was Astelle who came to his support. 'We must stay together,' she said firmly. 'I'm not afraid to take the risk and neither should you be, Graf.' Graf said no more.

After that, the next problem was getting a terrified Mig back onto the ice, especially since she had to hold onto Graf and Graf himself did not want to go. Once they were all holding on, the boots did the rest and in the end it was an experience they all enjoyed, speeding across the ice as the stars overhead faded into a rosy dawn which washed over them in pink and golden waves of light.

They climbed out onto the far bank of the lake, chattering and laughing. It was hard to believe now that such a short while ago they had been cold and miserable and almost without hope.

They gradually began to notice something that had begun very quietly all around them. Robert began to think that Gerrard's Zorgen was someone quite amazing if this too was his doing. As suddenly as the snow and night had fallen before, now day returned. The dawn light grew into bright sunshine. At their feet the snow began to melt and a carpet of green grass unfolded before them, scattered with bright flowers whose colours echoed the blue of the sky and the warm yellow of the sun.

Debbie, looking down at the flowers in delight, happened to glance at Gerrard's boots at the very moment that something strange happened to them. She saw the bright silver fade to grey, then darken into brown until they were the stout leather boots Gerrard had worn before. But the loss of the silver boots did not seem to matter then for the blossoming of the countryside around them seemed to say in a different way that what Gerrard had said earlier was true — everything was going to be all right.

Debbie had thought when she was cold and wet that she would want for nothing if only she could be warm and dry. Now that her jeans and sweater were rapidly drying out in the sunshine, she found herself feeling desperately hungry. It seemed she was not the only one for even as she thought longingly of roast chicken, potatoes, carrots and peas swimming in a thick gravy, Gerrard announced that they should think about getting some food before continuing their journey.

'Could we buy something from that village?' asked Astelle, pointing to a scattering of red-roofed houses clustered round a church just a short distance along the valley.

'If we had some money left we could,' said Gerrard wistfully.

'We've got money,' announced Graf shortly.

Gerrard looked at him in surprise.

'Thought it was stupid going into a cave full of treasure and coming out empty-handed,' continued Graf with a satisfied smirk. 'So I brought this bag of gold.' He reached to the belt at his side with an air of triumph. Then his face fell. 'It's gone!' he exclaimed in disbelief. He looked round at the others and his eyes fixed on Debbie. 'She took it!' he accused.

Debbie felt the colour drain from her face as all eyes turned on her. 'I don't know what he's talking about,' she protested.

'What do we know about her or her brother or that wild animal of theirs called a dog? Have you asked them where they're going or what they're doing here, Gerrard?' asked Graf with malice.

Debbie turned eagerly to Gerrard. Surely after their talk he could not think she had stolen the gold. But, as Gerrard met her gaze, she saw doubt cloud his eyes. 'Well, Debbie?' he asked.

'Please believe us,' Debbie found herself pleading, 'we're not here to steal. We came here to help someone — Princess Katherine.' As soon as the words were out of her mouth she wondered if she had said the right thing. Should she mention the note or the key? Words stuck in her throat. 'I don't know what he means about a bag of gold,' she finally managed to say, though her words sounded feeble in her own ears. She looked helplessly round the sea of curious faces and saw a strange expression on Kate's face.

'You mean King Bedien's daughter?' she asked.

'That's right!' agreed Debbie, trying not to sound surprised, trying to let Kate think that they had known before she told them that the Princess Katherine they were looking for was the daughter of King Bedien himself! Debbie glanced at Astelle to see if she would give herself away. But Astelle was looking curiously at Kate.

Debbie pulled out the damp pockets of her jeans. 'Look,' she said to Gerrard, 'You can see I haven't got anything.'

'She wouldn't have it on her, would she!' scoffed Graf. 'I reckon she'd hide it on the animal.'

Debbie's eyes darted to Chumley, standing alongside Mig, lapping the water from the edge of the lake. Gerrard moved to Chumley's side and Debbie held her breath as he touched the dog's collar and ran his hand through his fur. Chumley wagged his tail and Gerrard straightened slowly, holding in his hand the small bag of gold.

'Debbie didn't do it!' said Robert loudly before anyone else could say anything. 'I saw Graf take the gold when he should have been helping Gerrard rescue Kate.'

'Then *he's* in it with her!' pronounced Graf triumphantly, ignoring the accusations made against him.

'We can't prove anything,' said Gerrard looking solemnly at Robert and Debbie, 'but if either of you did take it, it would be better for you if you owned up now.'

There was a moment of uneasy silence. Finally Debbie looked at Robert. 'We didn't take it, Gerrard,' she said.

Gerrard was silent for a long while, then he sighed and shook his head.

'Gerrard, we cannot wait,' Astelle said firmly. 'We must travel on.'

Gerrard nodded and turned reluctantly to Debbie and Robert. 'I do not want to accuse you falsely, but you must see how things stand. Our journey is urgent. We must travel on — but we must ask you to accompany us no further.'

Debbie felt the tears prick in her eyes as she saw Astelle and Graf follow Gerrard. Kate, calling to Mig, paused to look at Debbie. Debbie thought she was about to say something when Astelle turned and asked, 'Are you coming, Kate?'

'Yes,' she said quietly and turned away.

Robert and Debbie stood watching until the others looked like dolls in the distance, nearing the village at the foot of the mountains.

'Robert, why wouldn't they believe us?' Debbie asked.

'They would have if we'd had the belt,' said Robert. He looked at Debbie and she could see that the same thought had struck them both.

'The breastplate! They've gone without it!' she said. Chumley, who had at first wanted to follow Mig, was now sitting on it. 'Chumley, get up quickly,' urged Debbie. 'We've got to hurry.'

They were still some distance away from the village when Debbie, looking up at the mountain, saw something which filled her with dismay. She saw Gerrard and the others coming out of the village onto the pathway which would take them up the wooded slopes at the foot of the mountain. Above them, hidden by a strand of tall pines, was a cloaked figure on a black horse. Beside him was another man, standing so that he would have a clear view of the four as they rounded a bend in the path. In his hands he held a bow, the strings taut and the arrow ready to fly towards its target.

Debbie froze in horror and the grim face of Edric came into her mind. She had forgotten the danger which threatened Katherine. What good was it being here in Mondar if all she could do was watch Katherine being ambushed and killed?

There seemed only one thing to do. She slipped the breastplate on and ran across the meadow towards the hidden attacker yelling at the top of her voice, 'Look out!'

Behind her Robert too yelled, 'Debbie! No!'

The men behind the trees turned at the sound of the shouting. It was then that Debbie saw what Robert had seen a few seconds earlier. Behind the cloaked figure and the archer, more armed men stepped out from behind the trees.

Debbie was too near to stop. She saw too late that she had put herself in danger but without drawing attention away from Katherine and the others. The black horse and its rider moved forward quickly through the trees. At the same moment the archer turned and aimed his bow at her.

Chapter eleven

Robert saw Debbie fall as an arrow hit her full in the chest. With heart beating fast he crouched down at her side. A second arrow split the air where he had been standing seconds before.

'Get down,' hissed Debbie. Robert looked at her in relief and surprise. 'I'm all right,' she whispered as Robert stretched out on the ground beside her. 'It only dented the breastplate.' Cautiously Debbie raised her head, partly screened already by Chumley who was covering her face with wet licks in appreciation of this exciting new game.

There was no one standing by the pine trees now. On the path where Debbie had last seen Astelle and the others, there were now men fighting. It seemed that some men from the village were putting the last of the attackers to flight. Gerrard was in the thick of the fighting but Debbie could see no sign of Graf. She was surprised, however, to see Kate and Mig come hurrying towards her over the grass.

'Debbie,' Kate asked breathlessly, 'are you all right?' As Debbie nodded, Kate smiled in relief. 'Thank you for what you did just now. You really . . .' Then she stopped, and a faint flush coloured her cheeks. Her next words took Debbie completely by surprise. 'You didn't take the gold,' she said 'I can see that now — you were telling us the truth. I'm really sorry I didn't believe you before. Can you forgive me, Debbie?'

'Well, yes of course,' said Debbie, embarrassed, 'But . . .'

'We're friends then,' said Kate, holding out her hand.

Debbie looked at her and felt that she was only now seeing her properly for the first time. It had seemed to Debbie that Kate was distant and unfriendly, that she looked down on Robert and herself. Now Debbie saw another side of Kate.

'Friends,' she responded, taking Kate's outstretched hand.

Kate smiled, then her eyes clouded. 'If you're both all right then, we'd better get back and help the others. They've taken Astelle. Some of the men are wounded and Graf has disappeared.' She turned away, leaving Debbie and Robert to follow, stunned by this news. As she turned away, Debbie thought she heard Kate mutter 'My fault,' but she could not be sure. In any case, one thought now blocked out all others from her mind: Astelle had been taken! If, as Debbie suspected, Astelle was really Katherine travelling in disguise, then she had been unable to help her after all.

When they reached the village a rosy-cheeked woman, plump and motherly, invited them into her house. She brought them bowls of savoury soup. 'They'll get her back,' she said. 'Don't you worry now. Just eat up.' Debbie, hungry as she had been before, now found she had no appetite at all.

'Do you think they'll find her, Kate?' she asked quietly.

Kate shook her head. 'I don't know.'

Robert looked up as he drained the last drop of his soup. 'Do you believe in Zorgen, Kate?' he asked.

Kate looked at him, 'Zorgen,' she said, 'I'm not sure . . .'

'Were you talking of Zorgen?' asked the woman, taking Robert's empty bowl from him. 'That breastplate looks to me like the workmanship of Zorgen. You sit by the fire and I'll bring you all a piece of my spiced cake and a cup of hot milk and honey.'

She turned to go and Robert touched her arm. 'What do you mean about the breastplate?' he asked.

She set the bowl down on the wooden table. 'Don't you know about the armour of Zorgen then?' she asked, smiling in surprise. 'Every child in the village knows that.'

'Oh yes,' said Kate. 'My father used to tell me . . .' She stopped suddenly, a faint blush touched her cheeks. 'But I've forgotten. Please tell us.'

'It's a suit of armour,' said the woman, settling herself down on a stool next to the children, 'but special, made with the powers of Zorgen for those who want to follow him. I know the metal, you see, because here in the village we have the shield. But, as I was saying, this armour, when you wear it, protects you. Not just from things you can see, you understand. From the things that get at you without you even realising they're there — from dark powers.'

Into Kate's mind as she listened to the woman talk, had come the scheming face of Edric. Then she remembered the moment of shock just now when, seeing Debbie wearing the breastplate, she had known Debbie had been completely innocent of stealing the bag of gold. She remembered too what Debbie had said about helping Katherine. The thought now came to her that perhaps Debbie was the writer of the anonymous letters. She had wondered at one time if they were written by Gerrard or even Graf but somehow she could not quite bring herself to trust them or Astelle. After all, when she first met them they had attacked her. Perhaps she could trust Debbie and her brother. She felt she desperately needed someone to help her reach her father, especially now that it seemed Edric had caught up with her. The ambush puzzled her. It looked as if Astelle had been taken in mistake for Kate herself. Yet Edric was far too clever to let his prey escape like that. There was something here she did not understand.

'And then,' the woman was saying, 'there's the key. Though, of course, that's not part of the armour!' Kate found her heart beating fast, not just at the mention of the key, but at the conspiratorial glance she saw Debbie exchange with Robert. The woman went on talking, unaware of the stir she had caused. 'The Key of Zorgen. It's a beautiful, little jewelled key and very important. Shows the king's in charge of Mondar while he's got that in his hands.'

'It's King Bedien we seek,' said Kate, interrupting the steady flow of words.

The woman looked at her in surprise. 'The king? Well, you won't find him easily. He's at a great conference in Pererin Palace. Difficult place to get to unless you've got someone like Red Rufus to show you the way.'

Kate, now unsure of Debbie and Robert, changed the subject quickly, thinking that later she would get the woman on her own and ask what she meant. 'I don't think we can do anything until we know what's happened to the others,' she said.

'No, of course not,' said the woman, sympathetically. 'But you can have a nice drink and a piece of cake.' She bustled away to get the promised refreshments while the children waited in an uneasy silence.

A large, blond man suddenly burst into the room, followed by Gerrard. 'No sign of them,' he said.

Gerrard looked at Kate and shook his head. Then he stiffened as he saw Debbie and Robert sitting on the nearside of the fire. The woman came hurrying in to greet her husband and, while they stood talking, Gerrard threw a frosty glance at Debbie and Robert. 'What are they doing here?' he asked Kate.

Debbie, her face pink with indignation, listened as

Kate explained to Gerrard what had happened. When she had finished he turned immediately to Debbie and Robert. 'Please forgive me?' he asked, his hazel eyes full of remorse. 'You have been very brave. I should have known you would not lie.'

At Gerrard's apology Debbie felt her face flush a deeper red with embarrassment. She was glad when he turned away to pick up the breastplate and examine it closely. Debbie watched curiously as the blond-haired man moved to Gerrard's side.

'The breastplate of Zorgen,' he said, his voice tinged with awe as Gerrard placed the breastplate in his hands. He fingered thoughtfully the embossed pattern which decorated its edges. The room was still in the mellow sunshine of the late afternoon. It seemed to Debbie that he was about to say something of great importance for them all.

The man turned to Gerrard. 'You do not need the breastplate now,' he said at last, 'but here in our village we have the shield of Zorgen. You must take it with you and find Red Rufus. He will guide you.'

Kate leaned across to Debbie and Robert and whispered. 'The man talking to Gerrard is Rodolph, the headman of the village.' She did not add that she had heard of Rodolph from her father Bedien. Neither did she add that the man called Red Rufus, that the headman had just mentioned, was rumoured to be a ruthless outlaw.

Rodolph brought the shield and his wife packed them some dark bread, slices of meat and honeycakes to take with them; along with chunks of meat and biscuits for Mig and Chumley. Then Rodolph solemnly presented Gerrard with the shield, which glinted and gleamed in the sunlight. 'May Zorgen go with you,' he said.

They left the village and struck out in the direction of some dense woods further along the valley where Rodolph had told them they would find Red Rufus.

Robert hung back behind the others. For some reason,

what the woman had said about the Key of Zorgen had stood out in his mind. He felt the urgent need to look at it and see if it was all right. He put his hand in his pocket and felt for the key. It was there. No one had noticed he had dropped behind. They were all looking at the distant woods and the flower-filled meadow stretching out before them. Furtively he pulled the key out of his pocket and placed it in his cupped hand. The gold and gems sparkled in the sunlight. As he looked at it the feeling stole over him that he should show it to Kate; that despite her tomboy clothes and manners, she was Katherine, the daughter of King Bedien.

At that moment, almost as if she could read his thoughts, Kate turned. Robert, looking up, saw her and read the look of shock and horror on her face. He heard her scream. It took him a few seconds to realise that she was looking not at him but at something in the air above his head and to realise that her scream was a warning. But by then it was too late for the key was torn from his hand. He looked up and saw an eagle soar into the air with the Key of Zorgen in his talons.

Above the woods, on the steep mountain slopes, someone else watched the eagle. As the great bird swooped down towards him, the cloaked figure stretched out his hand. He had seen the glint of gold between its talons and a slow smile touched his thin lips.

Chapter twelve

One minute the bird was silhouetted against the sun, the next, the sky was empty. Robert stood numb with shock, staring at his hand. A terrible, black feeling of failure swept over him.

Debbie and Gerrard, who had turned at Kate's scream, were running back to join Kate and Robert. 'What's happened?' Debbie called anxiously.

Kate looked at Robert and Robert looked at Debbie, stricken. 'It took the key,' he said.

'The Key of Zorgen?' Kate asked before Debbie could say anything. 'You had the key?'

Robert flinched at the accusation in her voice. 'Yes,' he said in a small voice. 'I'm sorry.' He flinched again at the anger that flared up in Kate's eyes. He went on talking even though she had turned away, her eyes following the direction of the eagle's flight. 'That's why we came here. To give the key to Katherine.'

Kate showed no sign of having heard him. 'Then Edric's got it,' she said dully.

Debbie, who had been shocked to hear Robert give their secret away to Kate, now stared as Gerrard went up to her and put an arm round her shoulders. 'Don't worry, Kate,' he said, 'we'll get it back.' He raised the shield in his other hand. 'We've got this and we've got Zorgen on our side.'

Despite his words Kate felt as if her heart had turned to stone. 'You don't know Edric,' she said.

'It's not Edric we have to fear,' Gerrard went on and paused, studying Kate's face as he wondered if she could take the news he had to break to her. 'It's Dolan.'

'Dolan!' exclaimed Debbie to Robert. 'That's the name in the note.'

'Dolan!' repeated Kate, drawing away from Gerrard in distress. 'But he's my father's friend. He's at the Peace . . .' She stopped suddenly, realising she had given herself away.

'It's all right. I know who you are, Princess Katherine,' said Gerrard, a teasing smile lighting up his hazel eyes. Kate's face showed no emotion as she looked steadily at Gerrard. 'I've been trying to protect you, Kate,' said Gerrard earnestly. 'That's why I wrote the notes.'

It was only then that Kate returned his smile. 'I'm glad it's you, Gerrard,' she said.

Debbie, who had been reeling from one shock after another, could contain herself no longer. She strode across to the couple she had been longing to find and had met without knowing. 'You wrote the letter!' she exclaimed in excitement. 'And you're Katherine!'

Kate and Gerrard turned to her as one, both with a look of surprise on their faces. 'It looks as if we've been hiding quite a few secrets between us,' Gerrard said, a smile breaking out on his face. 'What did you mean I wrote the letter?'

'That's what brought us to Mondar,' said Debbie excitedly, 'a note to . . .' Then she stopped and fished in the pocket of her jeans. 'Hang on. I've got it here. Oh . . .' Her excitement died as she drew out of her pocket a wadge of paper which bore no resemblance to the note she had found in the castle ruins. 'It must have got wet in the snowstorm,' she said, her voice dulled by disappointment.

'Look, Debbie, you can still make out some of it,' said Gerrard encouragingly, taking the note from her gently and prising it apart. Kate, peering over his shoulder, exclaimed in surprise to see the first letters of her own name. Words could still be made out here and there but only one sentence, broken and smudged, could be made out completely: 'Dolan seeks the key.'

'It's the note I lost, isn't it?' said Kate. 'The note that would have warned me.'

'I thought you'd read it,' said Gerrard. 'I thought that's why you ran away.'

'Why didn't you say anything when we met in the Far Woods?' asked Kate.

'I wasn't sure if Astelle and Graf were to be trusted. I didn't want to give them any clue as to who you really were or let them guess the reason I was hiding in the woods was to keep an eye on you. I couldn't risk them overhearing anything, And . . .' He paused, slightly embarrassed. 'I wasn't sure of you, especially when you arrived dressed in boy's clothes! I didn't know how you would react if I told you about the danger you and your father were in. I was glad that Astelle and Graf had said they were looking for Bedien and that you said you were too, because that gave me the excuse to travel with you.'

'Excuse me,' interrupted Robert abruptly, 'I don't think we've got time to stand round talking. All the explaining can wait till later. The key is gone. If Edric's got it . . .' He gave a shudder as he remembered Edric, '. . . we've got to get it back!'

Debbie looked at her brother in surprise. It was unlike him to speak so sharply.

'He's right,' agreed Gerrard, 'We've got to get the key. Whatever happens, we must stop it falling into Dolan's hands. Let's go.'

Debbie drew alongside Robert as they moved off. Despite his forceful words, he looked dismal. 'Are you all right?' she asked.

'I feel so bad about letting that bird take the key,'

he said.

'Don't blame yourself,' said Gerrard, overhearing Robert's words. 'How do you think I feel, letting those men take Astelle? Come on, let's find Red Rufus before it gets dark.'

Despite his attempt to cheer Robert, a worried look crept over Gerrard's face as he spoke. It was almost as if remembering the disappearance of Astelle and Graf and the loss of the key had cast a cloud over the recent discoveries they had made about each other. There seemed almost no point in going on.

Kate felt it too. Later she must find out how Robert had found the key in the secret tunnel, what he knew about it and what he had meant to do with it. She felt sure that she could trust Robert and Debbie after seeing Debbie wearing the breastplate, but she did feel annoyed that they had had the key and had not told her. Right now though, other things were foremost in her mind.

She reached absentmindedly to pat Mig. She was shaken by the news that Dolan, ruler of Calidon, whom she had supposed was her father's friend, was plotting to take Mondar from him. The fact that Astelle had been kidnapped and that someone — probably Edric — knew their movements and when to get the key, unnerved her. But most frightening of all was the thought that the Key of Zorgen might even now be in Dolan's hands. Kate shuddered. She understood now that if Dolan had the key, her father's life would be in the greatest danger. Mondar, the chief kingdom of the south, could have only one ruler — and that was the man who had the Key of Zorgen in his hands.

Suddenly Kate felt Mig stiffen beneath her hands. Mig arched her back and hissed, then tore herself away from Kate's grasp and bounded across the meadow. Chumley, barking furiously, followed her. The children looked at the animals in amazement, then saw beyond them what it was that had disturbed them. Silhouetted in golden evening sunlight was a man on horseback.

'Oh no,' murmured Debbie moving forward. 'Chumley, come back!' If this was the cloaked rider she had seen earlier then Chumley would be racing into danger.

What she saw next confused her even further. Mig and Chumley were still moving towards the dark rider but they had stopped hissing and growling. It seemed to Debbie that they were leaping and prancing forward effortlessly, at an amazing speed. She could make out Chumley's tail wagging furiously in delight. Then before she had taken that in, she saw something strange happen to Gerrard and Kate as they ran desperately after the two animals. Suddenly, instead of straining forward, they moved in graceful bounds, covering the distance between themselves and the rider incredibly quickly. Kate's delighted laughter floated back to Debbie as she stood poised with Robert at the edge of the long meadow grass.

'Do you think it's some kind of trap?' she asked Robert anxiously. 'Some kind of spell?'

'I'll let you know,' said Robert, bracing himself before stepping forward onto the grass.

'Robert!' Debbie shrieked. 'Be careful!'

Robert, as she watched, sprang into motion. She had never seen him run so easily. 'Come on, Debbie,' he called. 'It's wonderful!'

Debbie hesitated, then followed him. She felt the long grass close round her ankles as the red and yellow cups of the meadow flowers danced around her. Then it began. Her feet suddenly felt light, as if they had sprouted wings and, looking down, she saw that instead of her trainers she was wearing boots. They were as soft and supple as Gerrard's had been, but Debbie's, instead of being silver, were pale gold, like a field of waving corn. She let out a cry of delight. Then she forgot the boots as she let herself be lost in the wonderful feelings which wearing them had brought.

She felt energy surge through her. She wanted to run and leap and dance. But best of all, the meadow and the mountains and the sky grew bright and vividly beautiful. Everything that had before made her anxious no longer seemed to matter. This was Zorgen's world and Zorgen, Ruler of all, had power over everything in it. Bedien, the key, Astelle and Graf, the danger awaiting them from unseen enemies — Zorgen knew all about it and nothing would happen outside his perfect plan. Debbie found herself laughing as joyously as she had heard Kate laugh. And a new thought warmed her as she skipped through the meadow. As Zorgen would make everything all right in Mondar, so he would make everything all right at Polmar. She need not worry about anything. Zorgen had it all worked out for the best.

She found herself alongside Robert, alongside Kate. She saw that they too were wearing the boots. Kate's were leaf green, like sunlight shining through woodland trees. Robert's were deep blue, like a cloudless summer sky. Debbie pointed at their boots and they smiled at each other, calling out in delight as they moved after Gerrard towards the rider on the horse.

Debbie could see now that it was not the cloaked figure. The horse was white and the rider on it was a young man, dressed in armour except for his head which was bare, letting his hair take on the gold of the sun and the dazzling white of the reflected snow from the mountain peaks. He was smiling as they came towards him, enjoying their delight.

Gerrard, who reached him first, had recognised him for he called out 'Halien!' Then Kate let out a shriek of joy as she saw the small bird perched on his shoulder. 'Fleet!' she cried.

It was only when she drew closer that she saw Fleet had beneath his claws a familiar glint of gold and flashing colours. 'You've got the Key of Zorgen back!' she gasped. 'However did you do it?'

Debbie thought she was beyond being surprised but still she could hardly believe her ears when the bird opened its mouth and began to speak.

'Hello, Kate! I thought I'd never seen you again. I've been shut in a cage in the wood, trapped by Edric's men.'

'Oh, Fleet, I am sorry!' exclaimed Kate. 'Then how did you get here? And how did you get the key?'

'I found him and freed him, Kate,' Halien said.

'Kate,' said Fleet, 'This is Zorgen's son, Prince Halien. He rescued me in the wood and today saved me again.'

'Fleet risked his life,' said Halien, 'swooping out of the sun at the eagle. We were on our way to the Palace of Pererin when we saw the eagle with the key, flying towards the mountain.'

'Too proud that eagle was,' commented Fleet. 'Ignored me, you see. So, I surprised him and grabbed at the key!'

'But, my brave Fleet,' said Halien, 'the wound he gave you in pursuit was almost to the death.'

'Oh, Fleet!' breathed Kate. 'But — you're all right now?'

'All right? Kate, don't you know how Zorgen does things? He's made my song even sweeter. Put more power in my wings!'

Debbie looked at Robert. She had never heard of anything like this before. Then, as if to give a demonstration of the healing power which Zorgen had given to Halien his son, Fleet rose from Halien's shoulder to glide and swoop gracefully through the air, opening his throat in a burst of joyful melody.

'It's the same bird, Robert!' exclaimed Debbie. 'That's the bird I heard in the wood.'

Robert was watching Halien who was leaning low in his saddle, talking to Gerrard.

'Lose no time,' he was saying. 'Guard the key. Use the shield. Trust always in Zorgen, Gerrard.'

Fleet settled back on his shoulder as Halien pulled the reins of his horse and turned to face the wood. He gave them a last look over his shoulder, his eyes grave yet smiling. 'Kate. Debbie. Robert. May Zorgen go with you. Now farewell.'

They stood looking after him for a moment as the horse and rider galloped away till they disappeared from sight. Kate sighed. She turned to Gerrard. 'You know him well, don't you?' she asked wistfully.

'Yes,' said Gerrard smiling. 'I am his servant. It was Halien who sent me to seek you out, Kate — to guard you and to guide you.'

'Then he knew of this danger,' Kate said. 'Why couldn't he have stopped it? Why didn't he warn my father?'

Gerrard shook his head. 'I don't know. Zorgen sees what we do not see. His plans are perfect, but he lets us help him in his work, imperfect as we are.'

After that they were silent for a moment, each lost in their own thoughts. Debbie's eyes dropped to her feet. She was comforted a little to see that she still wore her boots.

'I know what they are,' said Gerrard, breaking into her thoughts.

Debbie looked at him puzzled. He smiled and indicated the silver boots which were once more on his feet. 'You were looking at your boots. I know what the boots are now. They're another part of the armour. Halien told me about them — he said they can take different forms, but they are always something which will help you walk as Zorgen wants you to walk.'

'We stepped into them when we came into the meadow, didn't we?' said Debbie.

'When we began moving towards Halien,' said Gerrard. 'And now we'd better do what he told us. Lose no time.'

It did not take them long to cross the meadow but as they stepped out of the flower-strewn grass onto the mossy soil at the edge of the wood, the dark shadows of the trees seemed to dim the joy and peace they had felt before. Glancing down, Debbie saw that, beneath a fading glimmer of gold, she had on her trainers once again. Then all other thoughts were swallowed up in a sudden feeling of fear. Faintly at first, then more clearly, she heard the clash of swords and the screams of men in pain. From the depth of the woods came the unmistakable noise of battle.

'They're attacking Red Rufus's camp,' said Kate fearfully to Gerrard. 'What shall we do?'

Before Gerrard had time to reply, Debbie saw a sudden movement from the trees behind him. A man stepped out armed with a sword. Gerrard whirled round. From the other side came another man. Chumley growled at one and Mig hissed at the other but it soon became clear that there were more of them — Dolan's men, seeking the Key of Zorgen.

Gerrard raised his head and gave a great shout as the men closed in on him. 'Help! In the name of Zorgen!'

Now a circle of armed men surrounded them. It seemed that they were doomed, for what could they do — unarmed, save for the shield, against men with swords and spears?

Suddenly, a cry echoed through the evening air and for a moment, made the men step back in fear. 'Zorgen . . . en . . . en!'

There, on his white horse, his helmet making him look fierce, was Halien. He cut through the circle so that the men backed away from the children and it seemed for a moment that all would be well.

The rider on the black horse came from nowhere. He was at Kate's side, his sword held at her throat, before any of them had realised what was happening. 'If you move, Halien, I'll kill the girl,' he hissed.

Kate closed her eyes in terror, her one last hope of rescue fading as she recognised Edric's voice. 'Now give me the key.'

Chapter thirteen

A fear gripped Kate so great that it put everything else out of her mind. She was aware only of the hard flank of the black horse behind her back and the cold blade of Edric's sword against her throat. 'He's going to kill me anyway,' she thought. Opening her eyes, she saw Gerrard, his face expressionless, holding out the key to Edric.

'Take it,' Edric hissed. The keen edge of the blade grazed Kate's throat. 'Princess Katherine,' came Edric's voice again, harsh with impatience. 'Take the key.'

Kate, her face white in the growing dusk, raised a trembling hand towards Gerrard who, in the act of handing her the key, seemed to be struck with sudden inspiration. He lifted the shield high and cried 'In the name of Zorgen!' As the words left his lips a blinding light flared out from the shield. It dazzled Kate and behind her, Edric. His grip on his sword relaxed for a moment and Kate, acting in reflex, dropped to the ground. The black horse reared in fright.

As suddenly as it had come, the light faded. Gerrard bent to see if Kate was all right. Debbie saw that Edric had regained control of his horse and was bearing down on Gerrard with raised sword.

'Gerrard!' Debbie screamed. 'Look out!' But her voice was lost in the noise of fighting which was breaking out around her as a band of armed men burst from the wood to attack Edric's men.

Edric's sword, poised in mid-air, was met by Halien's with a clash of steel. Edric, taken by surprise, was put on the defensive. So great was Halien's skill with the sword that it seemed Edric would soon be beaten. Debbie's heart leapt. If Edric surrendered the battle would be over. Then, to her horror, before she could even give a warning cry, she saw three of Edric's men attack Halien from behind. He swayed in his saddle, then slumped forward and toppled to the ground and Edric let out a shout of triumph.

Numbly Debbie pressed forward, trying to reach his side. She shook off Robert's arm as he tried to hold her back. 'He's dead, Debbie. Can't you see he's dead!' Robert cried.

One of Edric's men had pulled Halien's helmet off and he lay there with his open eyes unseeing and his face a lifeless mask. Debbie was suddenly shaken with a fierce anger against Edric even though he himself had not been the one to kill Halien. 'I hate you, Edric,' she cried, wishing she had a weapon to kill him herself.

To Robert's dismay it seemed Edric had caught his sister's words for his thin mouth broke into a ghastly grin and he turned his horse towards her. Seeing him, Debbie began to feel afraid.

'Edric!' a voice bellowed from behind her. 'Prepare to die!'

Debbie felt weak with relief. A burly man with a great bush of red hair and a thick beard pushed past her to lunge at Edric with his spear and unseat him from his horse. Debbie was close enough to see the sudden fear break out on Edric's face as he fell. Her own anger vanished as she saw the spear go into Edric and heard his dying scream of pain.

After that it was all over. Edric's men fled and the big

man turned to the four shaken children. 'Come,' he said, his round face stern behind his red beard, 'There's no time to lose.' He turned to Kate. 'Princess Katherine, we must go now — if we are to save your father Bedien.'

Kate's face turned pale as it had when Edric held his sword at her throat. She glanced at the still form of Edric sprawled on the ground, then nodded. 'Yes, Rufus. We are in your hands.'

Debbie and Robert moved uncertainly to join her but Gerrard, they saw, had crossed to where Halien lay in a pool of blood, darkening in the evening light. 'Gerrard!' called Kate. 'We must go.'

Gerrard turned, his face twisted with grief. 'I cannot leave my prince,' he said. He picked up Halien's helmet and turned it over slowly in his hands.

'Gerrard,' said Rufus sharply, 'are you abandoning the task which Zorgen has given you because his son lies dead?' He stopped abruptly, gritting his teeth in pain. 'You are needed now and needed quickly.'

Gerrard, straining to look at Rufus in the fading light, saw now that blood trickled from his left arm which he gripped tightly. Gently he closed Halien's eyes and placed the helmet by his side. 'In Zorgen's hands I leave you, my prince,' he said.

As Rufus led them along the shadowy forest paths up the lower slopes of the mountain, it became clear that he was quite badly wounded. Kate had bandaged his arm roughly but she could give him nothing to stop the pain. It seemed his left leg was also injured for, though he moved so quickly that the children could only just keep up with him, he walked stiffly and with a slight limp.

They did not have far to go. Cut into the hillside, but screened by trees and bushes, was a low cave. The children followed Rufus out of the twilight into pitch darkness. Debbie edged closer to Robert and Kate, straining to catch any sounds from the depths of the cave behind them. The sound of an owl hooting, inches away, made her jump. Almost immediately there was an answering call from the forest below. 'It's safe,' Rufus said.

Debbie saw, as Rufus lit a torch, that his face was grey with strain. She could see from the blankets and food stacked against one wall, that the cave had been prepared for their coming. Rufus bent to light the pile of wood set ready in the centre of the floor. 'We can have a fire just for a short while to warm us and to cook the food. Then we will sleep and in the morning I will take you to the path that leads to the Palace of Pererin.'

Debbie did not expect to sleep for the stone floor of the cave was hard and she dreaded the journey that lay ahead in the morning. She lay in the darkness, listening to Rufus moaning in his sleep. It seemed that he was not the only one who had been wounded in that battle. Gerrard, who had always been so strong and cheerful, now sat huddled in a blanket as if he had lost interest in his friends and surroundings. It was as if he had left them for some bleak world of his own. Kate, too, who had been ready to tackle anything, was quiet and withdrawn. Even the animals sat listless, close to the dying fire, as if someone had taken away their energy and simple joy in life.

In the morning they breakfasted quickly, then Rufus led them across the stony mountain and left them at a place beside a clump of pines where there was the beginning of a track that wound round the mountain out of sight.

The sun rose as they climbed and Debbie took her sweater off and tied it round her waist. Soon her turquoise T-shirt was clinging to her from the heat. She was glad at least that the climb took all their energy and that there was no need to talk. She wished more than once that they had the boots they had worn in the meadow on their feet now.

It was getting towards noon and they were attempting a particularly steep climb when Chumley, who had run on ahead, reached the top of the hill and started barking.

100

He ran back to Debbie, his tail wagging. With a renewed burst of energy Debbie scrambled up the slope to see what had made him so excited.

Gerrard was there first. He turned and called to the others, the signs of his old cheerfulness and enthusiasm lighting up his face. 'We've made it! The Palace of Pererin at last!'

Debbie gasped at the sight which met her eyes. Over the brow of the hill the rough, stony ground gave way to rich meadows, spreading across a wide plateau. In the centre of the plateau, against the backdrop of snow-covered peaks, lay the palace, its towers and pinnacles glinting in the sunlight.

Mig and Chumley ran off, bounding across the meadow until Gerrard called them back. 'We must be careful,' he said, 'We don't want Dolan to stop us before we can see the king.'

As they drew nearer they were surprised that there was no sign of any sentries on guard. The whole palace seemed deserted. There was a gatehouse but no guard. As they approached, the portcullis, which barred the huge gateway, opened before them. They looked at each other in surprise, then Kate and Gerrard stepped cautiously into the courtyard with Mig at Kate's heels. It was as Debbie followed that they began to discover why the castle had no need of guards. As Debbie stepped under the portcullis a loud, grinding noise startled her into stopping suddenly.

'Look out!' yelled Robert and flung himself at his sister so that they both fell forward onto the sharp gravel of the courtyard. The portcullis shuddered to the ground behind them within inches of Robert's heels.

Debbie picked herself up, more shaken than hurt. 'Thanks!' she said to Robert and bent to stroke Chumley who had rushed up to see what had happened.

Gerrard and Kate were walking across the smooth lawn, criss-crossed by gravel paths which met in a fountain at the centre of the courtyard. Debbie was disappointed that they had not turned back to see what had happened to Robert and herself. She discovered why when she followed them onto the lawn. It was as if she had stepped onto a giant sponge in a soundproof room. The grass beneath her feet was soft and springy, while the air around her seemed thick and very still.

Ahead of her, Gerrard suddenly shuddered and jumped sideways into the air. Kate, looking shaken, turned back to look at Debbie and gestured that she get off the grass onto the path. Debbie watched Kate leap for the path in several giant strides and did the same. As soon as she left the grass she was deafened by bursts of sound from everywhere — the crunch of gravel, bird-song, the rustling of leaves. Gerrard's voice sounded very loud as he called, 'Don't go on that grass again. It's booby-trapped. Some kind of shock just went right through me. In fact I think this garden is riddled with trick devices to stop intruders reaching the palace. I have a feeling now we should have brought Halien's helmet. I think that would have got us safely through.'

'Are we safe on the path?' asked Debbie.

Gerrard shrugged, then, trying to move forward, found it almost impossible to move his feet.

'Oh no!' exclaimed Robert, squelching up to join the others. 'It's like some kind of glue.'

Laboriously the children plodded along the path, coaxing the two bewildered animals along with them.

It was Gerrard, still walking ahead of the others, who discovered the next booby-trap. As he drew level with the fountain, jets of spray darted out from the fountain's rim and even from the path itself. All of them were soaked to the skin before they reached the far side of the fountain. But at least their wet feet moved more easily along the sticky path.

A wide expanse of gravel now separated them from the palace itself. Gerrard turned to the others. 'Wait here until I've made sure it's safe,' he said.

The same fear was in all their minds, that the worst

of the booby-traps would be set closest to the palace.
'May Zorgen protect you,' whispered Kate.

Gerrard smiled briefly at her then stepped forward
onto the gravel. To everyone's surprise and great relief
he crossed safely, arriving at the great oak door of the
palace. 'I'll knock,' he said hesitantly, wondering if they
had crossed the gravel safely only because the trap would
be triggered off by the door itself.

'Stop!' a voice called.

Gerrard, his hand lifted in mid-air, paused in astonishment as he saw Graf moving forward from the corner of
the building.

Graf lifted his finger to his lips, silencing all questions.
He motioned them to follow him.

'Gerrard,' whispered Kate as Graf turned away, 'can
we trust him?'

'I don't know,' Gerrard replied, frowning.

'Come on,' called Graf in a low, urgent voice, 'or it
may be too late to save Astelle.'

'Astelle is here?' asked Gerrard, moving forward.

Kate looked at Graf's thin face and touched Gerrard's
arm. 'Gerrard, let's find my father first,' she said.

They had rounded the corner now and Graf stood by
a small open door. 'This way. Quick!' he said.

'No,' said Kate. But even as she spoke, Mig, obedient
to Graf's command, had slipped through the doorway.

'I'm sure it will be all right,' said Gerrard. 'There are
four of us and we can be on our guard.'

'I'll take you to King Bedien first, if you like,' Graf
said to Kate.

Kate thought perhaps her suspicions were not very fair
and anyway there seemed no choice now. She stepped
through the doorway after Graf and followed him along
twisted corridors and up spiral stairs till he came to a
room overlooking the rear of the palace.

'I know this looks strange, but we need to keep out
of his way — the man behind Astelle's kidnapping. He
has his men posted everywhere. Stay here a minute while

I get you towels and dry clothes. Then we'll decide if you want to see the king first or Astelle.'

Gerrard moved to the window and looked out. Kate, stroking Mig, looked around the bare room. There was one bench beside the far wall. Debbie crossed to that and sat down with Chumley at her feet.

Robert, who had come in last, was still puzzled over something that did not seem quite right. 'Wait a minute!' he said, turning to Graf. He was in time to see the door swing shut and hear the bolt shot home on the far side of the door.

Chapter fourteen

Kate flung herself at the door and tried in vain to wrench it open. Gerrard had begun pacing the room, furious with himself for letting the others walk into a trap. Robert walked over to his sister and sat down next to her on the bench. 'I've just remembered something about Astelle,' he said.

Debbie looked at him glumly. 'I'm wet, tired and hungry. I'm fed up with Graf and Astelle and Zorgen and this whole stupid kingdom of Mondar. I wish we'd never come. Fat lot of help we've been. And now we're locked up in this room while Dolan is probably murdering Kate's father — and he'll be up here in a minute to murder us as well!'

Robert smiled. Debbie got like this sometimes. She'd been the same when they found out they had to move. But she usually came round after a while. 'There's one thing you've forgotten,' he said.

'What?' asked Debbie crossly.

'We've got the key,' said Robert.

'The key!' exclaimed Debbie loudly so that both Gerrard and Kate turned to look at her. 'We can use the Key of Zorgen to open this door!'

'Not with a bolt on the other side,' muttered Robert

under his breath. Kate, catching Debbie's enthusiasm, took the key and tried it in the lock. Of course nothing happened — except that Kate nearly lost it, for the key was so small in the large keyhole. She slipped the key on its chain back round her neck and grabbed the handle of the door, twisting and turning it in exasperation. The door opened and Kate, taken by surprise, lost her balance and fell backwards onto Mig. Debbie bent to help her up.

'Hello,' a voice said quietly. 'Are you all right?'

Robert stared in surprise as Astelle's heart-shaped face peered round the door, her forehead puckered with concern. He was glad he had not had the chance to say anything about her to Debbie, for it seemed she had now come to set them free.

Kate was back on her feet and all of them crowded round Astelle.

'What happened?' Gerrard asked. 'You managed to escape?'

Astelle frowned. 'Escape? I'm not a prisoner.'

'But you were kidnapped by Edric's men. Graf said you needed our help.'

'Oh, Graf!' Astelle said with a brief laugh. 'Take no notice of him. I wasn't exactly kidnapped, Gerrard.' She shivered as if at some unpleasant memory. 'I'll tell you about that later. Right now I want you to come with me to see King Bedien. He has been told the most dreadful lies about my father, Dolan.'

Kate gasped at the name Dolan but Astelle went on hurriedly, sorrow clouding her dark eyes. 'He's been told my father has been plotting against him. But that is nonsense of course. The plot is against Dolan. That is why I was travelling in disguise with Graf, trying to discover who was behind it.' She turned quickly to Gerrard. 'I'm sorry we had to lie to you, Gerrard. When we met you that day in the Far Woods, Graf and I pretended we too had only just met. Since we were in the woods near his castle, it seemed a good idea to say we were looking for Bedien. You understand that we could not risk telling you our real mission. You were a stranger and I did not know if we could trust you then.' She sighed. 'Anyway, I could discover nothing and now Bedien believes my father has stolen the Key of Zorgen.' She looked appealingly at Gerrard. 'You know what this will mean unless we prove him wrong. There will be war. Only we can stop it by placing the Key of Zorgen in Bedien's hands. Do you have the key?'

'Yes,' said Kate.

'No,' said Robert at the same time.

Astelle raised a dark eyebrow and looked from one to the other. 'Well?' she asked.

While Astelle had been talking, Robert's earlier doubts had returned. It seemed very clear to him that the only reason Astelle was setting them free was because she desperately wanted the Key of Zorgen. She was letting them out of this prison so that she did not need to take the key by force. Once the key was in Dolan's hands, they could easily be captured again — or worse.

'Well, Robert?' asked Astelle, laying her hand on his arm. 'Don't tell me you don't have the key.' Her lip trembled. 'I cannot bear to think what would happen were the key to fall into the wrong hands!'

Robert wanted to believe her. He looked round at the others, his face pink with embarrassment and confusion. Everyone else believed her. He was letting his imagination run away with him.

'I . . . er . . . I,' he stammered. 'I meant I haven't got the key . . . now.'

Robert was rescued from further misery by Gerrard who said briskly, 'Yes, we do have the key. We will go together to Bedien and then his own daughter can give him the key.'

Astelle's eyes widened as she followed Gerrard's glance. 'You mean Kate?' she asked.

'Yes, Kate,' he said.

Astelle hesitated then turned to lead them back down

the winding stairs, along corridors and then through a small walled garden. Kate followed eagerly, relieved that the adventure was almost over and that she was going to see her father at last. Then she heard the birdsong. Debbie heard it too and recognised it. She saw Kate's look of astonishment quickly turn into one of dismay.

Gerrard and Robert were ahead of them now, following Astelle through a doorway at the far end of the garden. As Astelle disappeared from sight Kate hurriedly removed the chain with the Key of Zorgen from around her neck. Fleet flew down and took it from her upheld hand.

'Debbie,' Kate whispered, 'there is something I must do. Can you see that Astelle does not know . . .'

'Yes,' said Debbie, nodding. 'You go. Don't worry. And, Kate . . .'

'Yes?' said Kate, as she and Mig turned back the way they had come.

'May Zorgen go with you.'

Kate smiled. 'And with you, Debbie.' Then she turned again and hurried along the path till the trees and shrubs hid her from sight.

Debbie caught the others up in the corridor. 'Sorry,' she said breathlessly. 'Chumley held me up. Kate will be along in a minute with Mig.'

'We'll wait here,' said Astelle.

'No,' said Gerrard, hoping he was doing the right thing from the face Debbie was pulling at him. 'I think we should press on. I'm sure they'll catch us up.'

Astelle looked doubtful and made a movement towards the garden door, but Gerrard, exchanging a quick glance with Debbie, was immediately at her side. 'We must get the key to Bedien,' he urged, taking her firmly by the arm.

'Yes, come on,' echoed Debbie, joining in the act and moving down the corridor.

'If Kate isn't with us when we get to the great hall, it'll be her own fault,' Gerrard said.

Astelle hesitated a moment longer, her eyes on Debbie's retreating back, then Gerrard felt her yield to the pressure of his arm. 'You're right,' she said. 'Let's waste no more time.'

Fleet's brief message had shocked Kate. Astelle had been lying. There was danger from Dolan. Fleet had already tried to warn Bedien but Dolan had stronger and darker powers on his side than they had suspected. Kate remembered how easily she herself had just been taken in by Astelle. Talking to Bedien would not be enough to convince him. It needed the power of Zorgen to do that. Kate had to bring her father not only the key but the great sword of Zorgen which she would find guarded in a place of many pathways on the north side of the palace. Kate wondered, with a sinking heart, as they came to the door leading outside, what this place could be.

She stepped out onto a magnificent lawn, sweeping away to the horizon, bounded by a semi-circle of thick pines and fir trees. Above them rose the snow-capped peaks of the mountains of Mondar. The view was breathtakingly beautiful but Kate spared it only a quick glance. Her attention was drawn to the huge green walls of a monstrous maze set on one side of the garden. Her heart sank. It must be at the heart of this maze that she would find the sword. Mig knew it too for she trembled and cowered behind Kate. 'You don't have to come, Mig,' Kate said. 'You can stay here and go for help if . . . if I don't come out.'

Mig arched her back, flexed her claws and put on a show of bravery for Kate. Kate smiled but her throat felt dry with fear. She and Mig stepped side by side into the high leafy opening and the green walls closed darkly in on them on either side.

Perhaps, thought Kate, there was no real danger. Perhaps the sword is guarded only by the feelings of fear created by the dark twisting leaves and branches reaching upwards to shut out the light of the sun.

She moved forward until the entrance to the maze was lost to sight. It seemed to her that the wall of the maze shifted, that very slightly the leaves and branches on either side of her moved so that she felt she would lose her sense of direction.

Nothing further happened and she began wondering if she had imagined the movement of the walls of the maze. She began to walk faster, gaining confidence as she rounded the next corner. So it was that the hidden menace of the maze caught her totally unprepared. Leaves, twigs and branches, inches to her left, suddenly formed into a leering, ugly face with sharp, pointed teeth. Below the face long twig-like arms ending in claw-like hands reached out for her, grabbing the ends of her long, red hair. With a scream she ducked down out of reach and stumbled forward. Another face, another set of hands reached out from the other side. Kate screamed again.

Ahead of her she saw that the maze walls were alive with hideous creatures who, if she stepped forward, would surely tear her apart. She jumped backwards, dodging the creature who had first attacked her, tumbled over a terrified Mig and went sprawling on the earthy floor. She lay there sobbing, angry and ashamed of herself, for her courage had completely deserted her. She could not go back to the palace without the sword but she could see no way of getting beyond the creatures who guarded the way forward. 'Oh, Mig,' she sobbed into her trembling cat's ear, 'what are we going to do?'

Chapter fifteen

Kate felt, before she saw, that there was someone standing beside her in the maze. A sudden feeling of peace washed over her. Not the feeling that she had had when the leaf-green boots were on her feet but a deep, comforting feeling that everything would be all right. She lifted her swollen eyes slowly and saw that a man in shining armour was standing at her side. She looked up into his face and a tremor of shock ran through her.

'Halien!' she gasped. 'But I saw . . .'

'You saw me die,' Halien said, smiling. 'Yes. It is true. You did. No, don't be afraid. I'm not a ghost. My father Zorgen is the Lord of life and he has power over death. At another time in another place I will tell you more; but for now just accept the fact that I am more deeply alive now than when you first met me.'

Kate blinked, trying to take it all in. She struggled to her feet. She could not understand what Halien meant but she felt the power and strength from him warming her through. She saw that he was holding his helmet out to her and, hesitating only a moment, took it from him.

'There is no time to lose, Kate. Put the helmet on. It will help you reach the sword at the centre of the maze in safety. Take it quickly to Bedien before it is too late.'

'Too late?' echoed Kate. 'What do you mean?'

But even as she spoke Halien disappeared and she was left alone with Mig in the grim, dark maze. A thin gnarled hand of leaves and twigs reached out to tear the helmet from her grasp. Kate took a hurried step backwards and put the helmet on.

Nothing changed. Kate bit her lip in disappointment. She adjusted the helmet on her head while the maze creature stared at her with green popping eyes and opened its jagged jaws wide in soundless laughter.

'It doesn't work, Mig!' Kate exclaimed in panic, 'and Halien's gone.' Mig looked pitifully at Kate. She too had felt the soothing calm when Halien was with them. He had given Kate this shining thing to cover her red hair. Surely Kate was supposed to do something now. Mig prodded her with a large paw. Kate looked down at her. 'Of course you're right, Mig,' she said. 'I have to go on and I'm supposed to hurry. Halien didn't say the helmet would make the danger disappear but he did say it would help me get to the centre of the maze.'

Kate's brave words helped her to step forward though it seemed the hardest thing she had ever done. The hedge in front of her immediately became alive with hideous creatures all turning their eyes on Kate and reaching out their claw-like hands towards her. Kate flinched but she kept moving. She came within reach of the first creature. A look of surprise, then anger distorted its face and it withdrew its clawing hands as if they had been stung. Gradually as she passed one creature after another without being harmed, her fears gave way as she realised that Zorgen was protecting her from harm.

It seemed as if she had been running down the leafy corridors of the maze for ever and at one time she wondered if its trick of shifting and changing shape was leading her away from the centre. Then suddenly, when she was hot and tired and beginning to lose heart, she rounded a hedge and came upon a small clearing. She was sure straight away that it was the centre but her heart sank for there was no sign of a sword. There was only a particularly prickly bush intertwined with thorny creeper.

'Zorgen,' she asked urgently, 'where is your sword?' In the centre of the maze. She had already been told that. She looked at the bush and she knew then what she had to do. 'Zorgen, help me,' she whispered and, before she lost courage, she plunged her hand into the thorny bush.

Her hand brushed against a branch covered with vicious thorns. She narrowed her eyes and braced herself against the pain. Nothing. She opened her eyes wide to find that the thorns and leaves were curling in on themselves as if afraid of human touch. She let out a sigh of relief and began tearing the creeper aside until she had parted the bush and could glimpse the jewelled hilt of the sword. She drew it out and held it high. It flashed silver in the sunlight and the whole clearing glowed with dancing green and golden light. Kate had the Sword of Zorgen in her hand.

Meanwhile, Debbie was beginning to get anxious. She was running out of excuses to give Astelle. They had not yet reached Bedien's rooms and Astelle was growing more suspicious by the minute. Suddenly Astelle stopped and turned. 'I'm going back. Kate can't possibly have taken this long with Mig. I'm going to find her.'

'No, wait a minute, Astelle,' cried Debbie, stepping in front of her.

'Out of my way,' Astelle said, sweeping past her. There was no friendliness left in the cold gaze she gave Debbie. 'You will all wait for me here,' she said frostily as she paused to knock on a door further down the corridor.

The young man who came out put his hand to his sword-hilt when he saw Gerrard and Robert. Astelle, laying her hand on his arm, said something to him in a low voice. An arrogant smile played on his lips as his eyes passed over the three children, then he turned on his heels and followed Astelle down the corridor.

Robert, watching them move away, wished he had finished warning Debbie about Astelle. He had been going to tell Debbie about the aura of evil he thought he had glimpsed round Astelle in the cavern, but then he had been taken in again by her beauty and charm.

Gerrard looked at Debbie's stricken face. 'What's going on?' he asked.

Debbie told him as briefly as she could about Fleet's visit to Kate and what Kate had asked her to do. She found herself pouring out her anxiety about the danger Kate was in.

Gerrard cut Debbie off abruptly. 'Yes, I know all about the danger. Don't forget I'm the one who wrote the note. Now, where do you think she's gone?'

Debbie flushed with embarrassment. She had been silly to try and handle things alone. She should have remembered who Gerrard was and how he had been Halien's friend and servant. 'I don't know,' she said lamely, 'but back through the garden anyway.'

They found Fleet in the garden and Gerrard understood his message. 'To the maze,' Gerrard said, running across the garden. 'She's gone into the maze.'

Kate was at that moment coming out of the maze again. Her relief to round the last corner and glimpse the lawns ahead was cut short as two figures stepped suddenly into the opening, blocking out the light. Kate gasped in alarm. One of them was Astelle, her eyes blazing. The other was Armard. Kate tightened her grip on the sword and hoped that she was not going to have to use it. She saw Armard raise his sword, remembered Marise's tales of his great skill, and shivered.

It was then that Mig's hour of glory came. She had felt bolder and braver than she had ever felt before as she had followed her mistress past the terrifying creatures of the maze. It seemed to Mig almost as if the smiling young man who had given them his helmet had stayed

114

with them, protecting them every step of the way. He would protect them now. Mig soared into the air, her powerful body moving forward at lightning speed, and landed with both paws full on the chest of the astonished Armard. Astelle retreated quickly as Armard crashed to the ground with an impact that sent his sword flying from his hand. Astelle, her eyes fixed on Mig, stepped straight into Gerrard and Robert's waiting arms.

Kate, weak with relief, patted Mig then ran to Gerrard's side. She reached him as Gerrard picked up Armard's fallen sword and held it against Astelle. 'Take me to the King,' he said sharply, 'and no more tricks.'

The lords of Mondar were gathered in the great hall when the children burst past the astonished guards into the room. Bedien rose immediately from his place at the head of the great table, drawing his sword from its scabbard. 'What is the meaning of this?' he asked sternly.

'Father!' cried Kate, running forward. Bedien stared at the figure in the rough, crumpled clothes running down the hall towards him. He gasped in astonishment as she pulled off the helmet, letting her red hair fall about her shoulders. 'Kate!'

Kate flew into his arms and closed her eyes briefly as she leaned against his chest, safe at last. 'Kate,' Bedien said again softly. 'I'm glad to see you.' He held her from him to examine her pale, dirt-stained face, 'But why are you here?'

Kate turned from him to study the two rows of great lords, sitting at the table watching the scene before them in astonishment. She looked for Dolan. Dolan returned her gaze, his expression no different from that of the others around him except that, as her eyes met his, he smiled. Dolan, her father's friend. Was it really true that he was her father's enemy? She looked at Astelle and wondered if she had also been lying when she said Dolan was her father.

'Kate?' her father asked.

Now that the moment she had waited for had come, Kate found she was not sure what to say. She turned to look at the others.

Gerrard saw the bewilderment in her face and came forward. He cast a puzzled glance at Kate, wondering why she hesitated, then knelt before King Bedien. 'We bring you the Sword of Zorgen, your majesty,' he said. 'We believe you may have need of it for we come to warn you of treachery,' he paused and looked from Bedien's astonished face to the Lords seated round the table, 'from one who sits in conference here . . .'

Until now, a waiting silence had filled the great hall while motes of sunlight filtered in through the high arched windows. Now the sound of voices broke out around the long table: protests and exclamations of surprise and anger.

Kate's eyes were on Dolan. His face was calm but a flicker of anger burned in his eyes. 'My Lords,' he exclaimed in a powerful voice which rose above all other sounds. 'Let us be calm. We are rulers of duchies and kingdoms. Shall we behave like the lowest of our subjects on the words of a mere boy? Bedien, king of Mondar, the greatest kingdom amongst us, must judge if this boy speaks true or if he lies to bring quarrelling and division among the kingdoms.'

His reasoned words made sense. Kate looked at her father but could not read his expression. She looked at Gerrard and saw his face darken with anger. Finally she looked at Dolan and saw the hint of a smile which vanished even as she looked.

'This is a grave accusation you make,' Bedien said. 'Have you proof against the man you accuse?'

The colour rose in Gerrard's face and Kate saw that he was finding it difficult to answer. It was then that she knew for certain that Dolan was the traitor they had believed him to be. He was a clever man. If he was not, her father would not have been deceived by him for a moment. His carefully chosen words drew the finger of

116

suspicion away from the lords sitting at the table and from himself. It pointed now at Gerrard instead.

'Father,' Kate broke in urgently. 'Please take the sword.' She knew now that only the Sword of Zorgen would help Bedien see where the truth lay. She held out the hilt of the sword to him.

Bedien, with a look at her anxious face, reached out his hand for the sword.

'Wait!' called a voice from the back of the hall. 'Do not touch the sword, my Lord King.'

All heads turned as Astelle came hurrying forward. 'The sword is stolen from the centre of the maze. Beware the evil power of that sword!'

Astelle's hasty words could well prove her father's undoing, Kate thought with relief. Kate saw the angry flush colour Dolan's cheeks as he stared at his daughter. Astelle, in trying to outwit Gerrard, had given away how much she and her father feared the power of the sword.

It seemed Astelle's words had affected Bedien in the same way for he took the sword. He turned the jewelled hilt over in his hands wonderingly, then lifted his eyes to look at Dolan.

Dolan had known what Bedien would see when he took the sword. Before anyone had realised what he meant to do, he had leapt from his place and had run at Bedien with his own sword raised.

What Bedien saw was Dolan as he really was; cruel, ruthless, scheming, driven by a force of evil so terrible that it left Bedien feeling sick with shock. Shaken by the horror of his discovery, Bedien was caught unprepared by Dolan's attack. He raised his sword just in time to meet the biting steel of Dolan's blade.

Bedien stumbled, then struggled to regain his footing as Dolan came at him again. Around the room the guards and the lords who could have rushed to his defence waited with bated breath. They all understood, without being told, that the struggle must be between Dolan and Bedien alone: the treacherous lord behind whom the forces of darkness gathered and the king who fought for Zorgen with the power of Zorgen's sword.

Kate could hardly bear to look. Her father had struggled to his feet while parrying Dolan's fierce attacks. 'Zorgen, help him,' she whispered. The dangers of the journey, the horror of the creatures in the maze, they were all nothing now beside her mindless fear for her father's life.

Chapter sixteen

Sunlight blazed stronger than before through the high arched windows and the sword of Zorgen caught its fire. Bedien felt the power of Zorgen pulse through the sword, pure and strong like the sunshine. With beads of sweat breaking out on his forehead, he wielded it so that it flashed through the air, striking again and again against Dolan's blade till a powerful blow sent the sword spinning out of Dolan's hands. Bedien looked sternly at the man who had pretended to be his friend and held the point of the Sword of Zorgen against his heart.

Astelle rushed forward, sobbing hysterically. 'Don't kill him! Your Majesty, I beg you, spare his life.'

Dolan himself fixed his hard cold eyes on Bedien's face and said nothing. Kate shivered as she saw the hatred in his eyes. Then, looking at her father, she was moved to see a mixture of sorrow and pity in his eyes as he met Dolan's gaze. 'Did you think you could win against Zorgen, Dolan?' he said. Then, in a heavy voice, he called, 'Guards! Take King Dolan to the dungeons. Lock the Lady Astelle in the North Tower.'

It seemed then that it was all over. Kate felt weak with relief. Then, as Dolan was marched away between two guards, he passed Astelle, who spoke to him hurriedly. A smile of triumph crossed his face.

'Wait!' he called. 'I question the authority of Bedien to pass judgement on me. He claims to be Ruler of Mondar. Can he produce the Key of Zorgen?'

The guards stopped, confused. Bedien turned to look at Kate, in whose care he had left the key. 'Fleet has it,' whispered Kate, 'but I don't know where he is.'

Debbie, who had watched the events of the past minutes in stunned silence, might at this moment have felt dismayed, knowing that Kate no longer had the key. Instead she felt excited. The Key of Zorgen was needed urgently to save Mondar from the scheming plans of Dolan. All the discomfort and danger seemed worthwhile, for this, at last, was the moment for which Zorgen had brought them into Mondar. Debbie alone, out of all the people, who waited tensely in the great hall, looked up to the open windows and saw exactly what she had expected to see; Fleet, flying in with the golden chain in his claws. Hanging from it, sparkling with rich lights, was the Key of Zorgen.

Debbie smiled as Kate looked up, startled, when Fleet landed on her shoulder. She saw Bedien's mouth widen in a smile of relief as Kate put the key into his hands. She looked at Robert who was smiling too. 'I think that's Dolan done for,' she whispered.

Robert shifted his glasses up the bridge of his nose. 'About time too!' he said.

Afterwards in Bedien's apartments, there was a celebration feast. Many were the exclamations of delight and surprise as each of the children told their part of the story.

Debbie's embarrassment that she had been so completely taken in by Astelle, was tinged with relief that everything had worked out all right in the end. Astelle had not got away with her heartless scheming.

The arrival of Armard had been a surprise for Kate. It seemed that it was only thanks to Fleet that Kate had escaped the clutches of Armard and his fellow plotters earlier. When Astelle and Graf had arrived at Bedien's castle it was to meet with Edric then wait in hiding until Armard could bring them the key, which all three of them would take to Dolan. Marise had been searching Kate's room. If she could not find the key, it had been decided that other means would be used to make Kate disclose its whereabouts. But then Kate had run away. This had not worried the plotters unduly because they knew that Astelle and Graf were lying in wait in the woods. What they had not realised was that Gerrard was there too. His presence had foiled their plans. Kate was glad that she had been blissfully unaware of all the traps which had been set for her. She had found the adventure in the maze dangerous enough!

The others sat wide-eyed as Kate related what had happened. When she had finished Bedien hugged her to him. 'My brave Kate!' he said. Gerrard could only stare at her, an expression of hope mingled with wonder on his face. 'Halien is alive?' he repeated.

'Yes,' said Kate, who had forgotten what a surprise this would be for the others.

'You're sure?'

'Yes. It's true! I could hardly believe it myself at first but it *was* Halien! He talked to me, Gerrard. He gave me his helmet. He told me his father, Zorgen, has power over death. I don't understand it, but I *know* it happened.'

Then it was Gerrard's turn to surprise them. He gave a great shout of joy. 'Alive! Halien's alive!' He seized a startled Kate by the hands and waltzed her round the room. The others laughed. Then slowly it began to dawn on them what an amazing thing it was that the son of Zorgen had conquered death itself.

'We will talk of this tomorrow,' Bedien said solemnly to Gerrard, 'but now we must get Robert and Debbie home.'

Strangely enough it had not occurred to Debbie until

121

then that, since they had seemingly wandered into Mondar by chance, there was no obvious way in which they could return home. She also realised, with a pang of guilt, that she had not given a thought to how worried her parents must be.

'Come,' said Bedien smiling and holding out his hands to Debbie and Robert. 'I will take you along the corridor of untravelled time.'

Debbie turned to Kate and Gerrard.

'Thank you, Debbie, for all you've done — and you too, Robert,' said Kate, stepping forward to give Debbie a quick hug.

'Goodbye,' said Debbie, struggling to keep back the tears which had suddenly sprung to her eyes.

'Zorgen go with you,' Gerrard called as they moved away.

'Zorgen be with you too,' said Robert. 'Bye, Mig.' Mig gave a small mew of distress as Chumley moved away after Robert. The strange animal she had disliked on first sight had become such a good friend.

'We must hurry,' said Bedien, leading them out into the corridor and up a flight of stairs. At the top of the stairs they came to a halt, for the way was barred by a huge door. It was made of a strange wood which seemed to catch the light from the windows set in the walls on either side of it, so that it seemed at one moment blue, the next grey, the next dappled with sunlight. It was almost as if it was made out of a piece of sky. Halfway down on one side of the door was a small key-hole. Into it Bedien put the Key of Zorgen and turned it softly in the lock.

It seemed as if the door melted away rather than swung open and Robert and Debbie found themselves walking on a carpet of white cloud along an arched corridor of sky. In the walls of the corridor there were doors set at intervals.

'The doors open to worlds beyond Mondar,' Bedien said. Debbie nodded speechlessly, dazzled by what she saw. 'Let me show you,' he continued and, pausing at a door, opened it with the Key of Zorgen.

Robert and Debbie peered cautiously through the opening and gasped in wonder. The door opened into space. Everywhere stars twinkled in a sky of deep, velvet blue — except for one part directly ahead of them. There the domed roofs and pinnacles of a glistening city in space sparkled and shone in a rainbow of colours. Bedien closed the door, smiling at the dazed expressions on their faces. 'Not everywhere is like Mondar — or Earth,' he said. 'But this place,' he continued, moving on and pausing to unlock another door, 'is like nowhere else you will ever see!'

Debbie thought at first glance she was looking at Earth and she was disappointed. She saw grass, trees, flowers, lakes, rivers and mountains. Then she found that as she looked she could see more and more places, all breathtakingly beautiful, all completely different. The colours were pale and lovely or rich and deep, but always satisfying, a delight to look at. There was nothing anywhere that could be made better in the smallest detail. Everything was exactly right.

All this Debbie realised in the first few seconds before she noticed that everywhere there were people. They seemed busily occupied, though she could not see what they were doing. They talked and laughed and some, she thought, sang as they worked. She could see them clearly but not hear them.

One face turned towards them, smiling, and a shock of recognition passed through Debbie. Surely that was Halien! Not as she had last seen him, his face grey and his eyes glazed, but bubbling with life, colour in his cheeks and his eyes sparkling with joy. Then a rich, golden light poured over everything, so bright that Debbie had to turn away. Gently Bedien closed the door. 'Zorgen's kingdom,' he said.

'We won't be there tomorrow when you tell Kate and Gerrard about Zorgen,' Debbie said wistfully.

Bedien paused then pushed the third door wide open. 'This is where you can learn best about Zorgen,' he said. 'This is where he wants you to serve him. Step through the door, Debbie.' He released her hand. 'And you, Robert. May Zorgen be with you both.'

Through the doorway was a carpet of green grass, spread with summer flowers and above it the clear, bright sky of early morning. Debbie stepped forward gingerly. The grass beneath her feet felt like grass. A light breeze touched her face. She turned back to say goodbye to Bedien and to thank him. Behind her stood Robert looking about him in wonder and behind him, Chumley, eagerly sniffing the air. Behind Chumley was the wood that days ago they had wandered through and stumbled into adventure.

'We're home,' said Debbie in a shaky voice and then, to Chumley's surprise and Robert's dismay, she burst into tears.

'It was because I felt happy and sad at the same time,' explained Debbie later as they walked behind their parents into the village that afternoon. To their amazement and relief their parents had still been in bed fast asleep when they arrived home. They could hardly believe that after all that had happened they were home again in the same morning of the same day only minutes later than the time they had stepped into the wood. Such was their relief that they did not even mind going to the Throwers' for tea.

The Throwers' house was large and modern. Mrs Thrower opened the door to them, smiling, and made a big fuss of Chumley. 'Don't worry if Fuzz spits at you,' she said to Chumley. Then to Debbie, 'Fuzz is our cat.' A small, black cat appeared as if on cue. Its fur bristled at the sight of Chumley and its tail bushed out before it shot like an arrow up the stairs. Chumley wagged his tail, staring after it with interest.

'Come on in,' Mrs Thrower was saying. 'I expect

you'd like Emily to show you where the computer is, Robert. Debbie, Katherine's been dying to meet you.' Robert's eyes lit up at the word 'computer'. He did not hear the name Katherine mentioned or see the startled glance Debbie threw at him.

'Now, I wonder where's she's got to,' said Mrs Thrower, leading them into the large, comfortable living room with French windows opening out into the garden. 'Oh, there she is! With the rabbits. I should have guessed. You go on out, Debbie.

Mrs Thrower opened the French windows wide and called out 'Kathy, here's Debbie!'

Debbie stared at the slim figure with short, brown hair at the bottom of the garden. Kathy not Kate. For a minute there Debbie had thought . . . Silly, really. Mondar was another world in a different time and place.

'There are other worlds, different from Earth and Mondar,' Bedien had said. Then, as they stepped back into their own world he had told them, 'This is where you can serve Zorgen.'

Debbie, moving towards Kathy through the summer garden, saw it all very clearly for a moment. How, beyond this world there was a deeper, richer world and yet this world was part of it. Zorgen's world it was called in Mondar, but in church, her father called it God's world.

Then, as suddenly as it had come, the idea slipped away again in the short time it took Debbie to reach Kathy, who was holding out a rabbit for her to stroke.

'This is Smoky. Hold her if you like.'

The rabbit looked at her with large, dark eyes. Debbie took it shyly from her. 'Hello, Smoky,' she said to the rabbit.

There was a moment's awkward silence while Debbie and Kathy searched for something to say.

'I thought,' said Kathy finally, 'that I could show you round next week if you like. There are some interesting places round here. We could cycle out to Polmar Tor.'

125

'Yes,' said Debbie smiling. 'I've been there, but I'd quite like to go again.' It would be fun, she thought, to go to Polmar Tor with Kathy. There would be no going to Mondar, of course. There was no need to go there now.

There was another silence while the girls looked at Kathy's rabbits. But this time it was a comfortable one. The kind of silence that can be shared by friends.